Journey to the Center of the Earth

Jules Verne

SADDLEBACK
EDUCATIONAL PUBLISHING

Saddleback's *Illustrated Classics*™

SADDLEBACK
EDUCATIONAL PUBLISHING
www.sdlback.com

ISBN-13: 978-1-56254-914-5
ISBN-10: 1-56254-914-6
eBook: 978-1-60291-156-7

Printed in Guangzhou, China
NOR/0713/CA21301348

17 16 15 14 13   4 5 6 7 8

Welcome to
Saddleback's *Illustrated Classics*™

We are proud to welcome you to Saddleback's *Illustrated Classics*™. Saddleback's *Illustrated Classics*™ was designed specifically for the classroom to introduce readers to many of the great classics in literature. Each text, written and adapted by teachers and researchers, has been edited using the Dale-Chall vocabulary system. In addition, much time and effort has been spent to ensure that these high-interest stories retain all of the excitement, intrigue, and adventure of the original books.

With these graphically *Illustrated Classics*™, you learn what happens in the story in a number of different ways. One way is by reading the words a character says. Another way is by looking at the drawings of the character. The artist can tell you what kind of person a character is and what he or she is thinking or feeling.

This series will help you to develop confidence and a sense of accomplishment as you finish each novel. The stories in Saddleback's *Illustrated Classics*™ are fun to read. And remember, fun motivates!

Overview

Everyone deserves to read the best literature our language has to offer. Saddleback's *Illustrated Classics*™ was designed to acquaint readers with the most famous stories from the world's greatest authors, while teaching essential skills. You will learn how to:

- Establish a purpose for reading
- Activate prior knowledge
- Evaluate your reading
- Listen to the language as it is written
- Extend literary and language appreciation through discussion and writing activities.

Reading is one of the most important skills you will ever learn. It provides the key to all kinds of information. By reading the *Illustrated Classics*™, you will develop confidence and the self-satisfaction that comes from accomplishment—a solid foundation for any reader.

Step-By-Step

The following is a simple guide to using and enjoying each of your *Illustrated Classics*™. To maximize your use of the learning activities provided, we suggest that you follow these steps:

1. ***Listen!*** We suggest that you listen to the read-along. (At this time, please ignore the beeps.) You will enjoy this wonderfully dramatized presentation.

2. ***Post-reading Activities.*** You have successfully read the story and listened to the audio presentation. Now answer the multiple-choice questions and other activities in the Study Guide.

Remember,

"Today's readers are tomorrow's leaders."

Jules Verne

Born in Nantes, France, in 1828, Jules Verne was the son of an attorney. His father expected him to become an attorney, too, but Verne was addicted to sea travel and scientific study.

Jules Verne was at his peak as a writer of science fiction from 1862 to 1872. In fact, many of the creations of his fantasies described in his books were later actually invented. Submarines, for example, were used by Verne before they were manufactured. In the nineteenth century, Verne was talking about rockets around the moon, television, atomic bombs, polar travel, photography, automobiles and travel to the center of the earth.

Many of his scientific discoveries are embodied in his books. Two of the best known are *20,000 Leagues Under the Sea* and *Around the World in Eighty Days*. Twenty-nine years before the Wright Brothers achieved powered flight, Jules Verne, in his imagination, had sent a rocket to the moon in his story *From Earth to the Moon*. He also wrote *The Castaways of the Flag, Five Weeks in a Balloon, Master of the World,* and *Mysterious Island*.

Jules Verne died in Amiens, France, in 1905.

Jules Verne

Journey to the Center of the Earth

Henry Lawson

Hans

Professor Von Hardwigg

Dr. Fridreksson

Gretchen

At one hundred miles inside the earth, we discovered a giant forest, a herd of prehistoric mastodons, and a giant shepherd tending them! We hid behind a tree, fearful of being discovered.

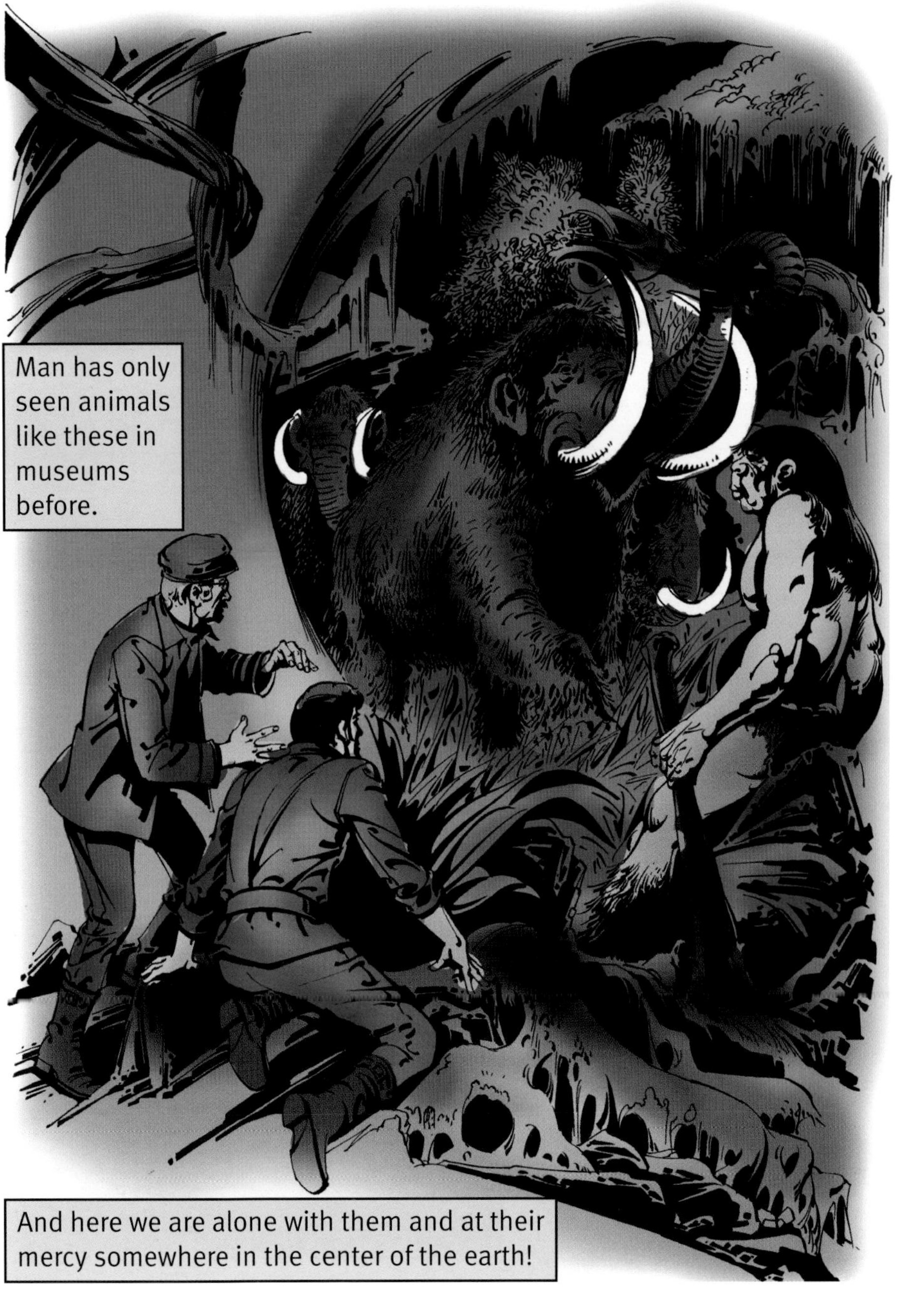
Man has only seen animals like these in museums before.
And here we are alone with them and at their mercy somewhere in the center of the earth!

My strange adventure began in the 1860s in the city of Hamburg, Germany. There I lived and studied with my uncle, Professor Von Hardwigg—a famous scientist interested in minerals and geology.

I can learn everything about the earth from Uncle if I work hard.

Uncle had a beautiful goddaughter whom I hoped to marry.

And everything about heaven from my beloved Gretchen!

Uncle was a very smart man . . . and also impatient!

Henry! Henry! Henry!

Uncle is home!

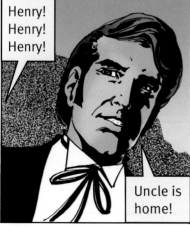

Henry are you coming up?

Coming, Uncle!

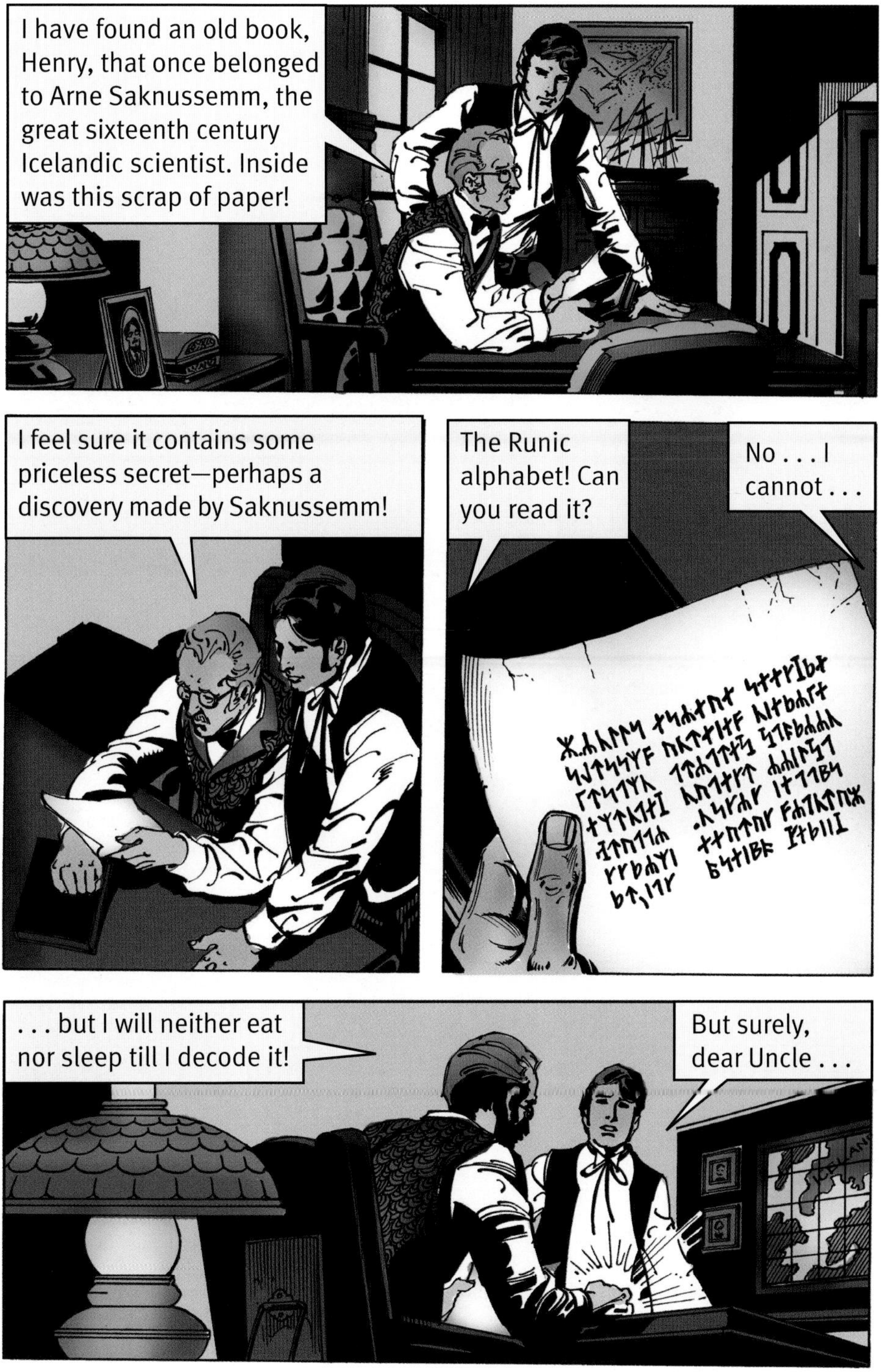
I have found an old book, Henry, that once belonged to Arne Saknussemm, the great sixteenth century Icelandic scientist. Inside was this scrap of paper!
I feel sure it contains some priceless secret—perhaps a discovery made by Saknussemm!
The Runic alphabet! Can you read it?
No . . . I cannot . . .
. . . but I will neither eat nor sleep till I decode it!
But surely, dear Uncle . . .

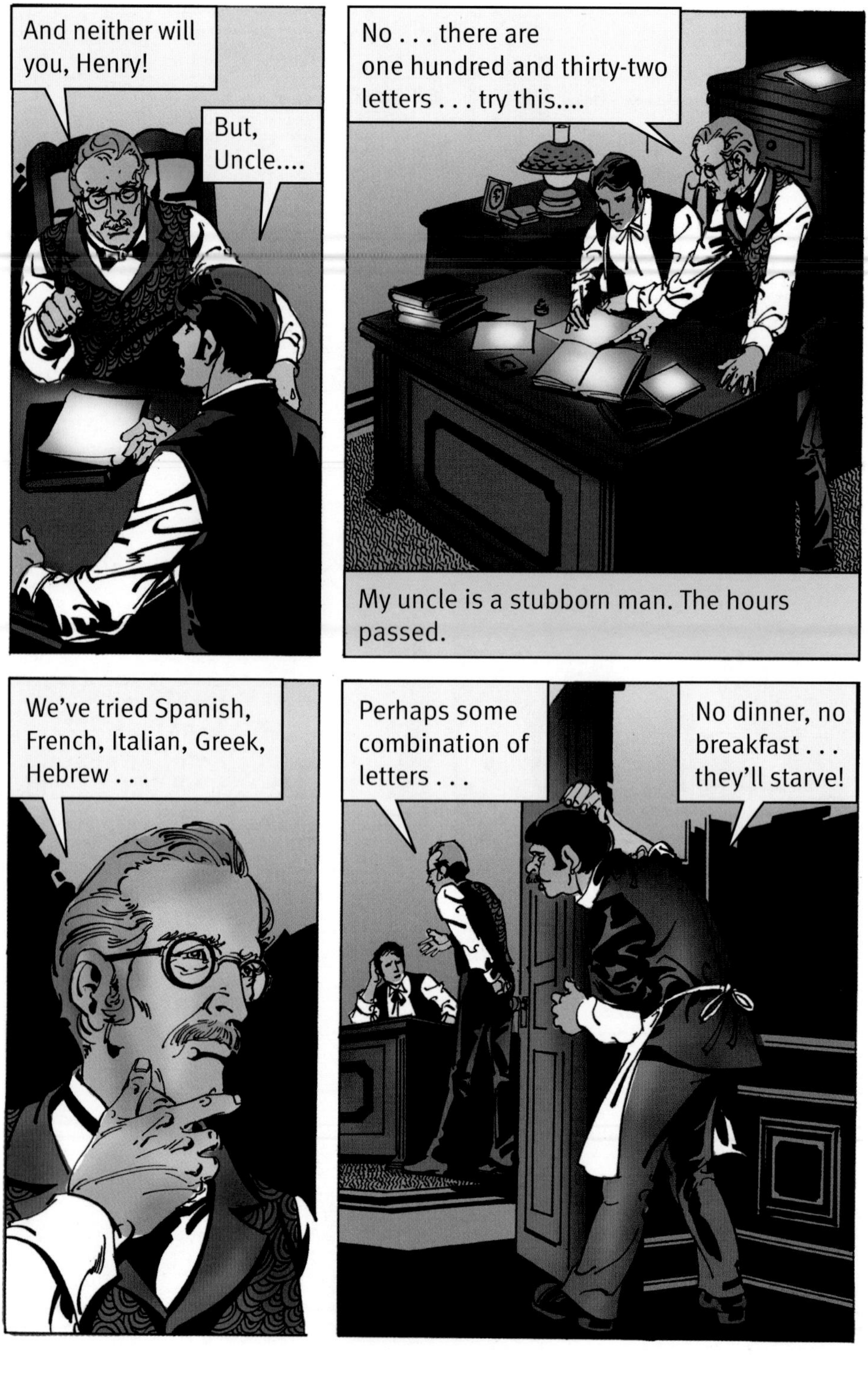
And neither will you, Henry!
But, Uncle....
No . . . there are one hundred and thirty-two letters . . . try this....
My uncle is a stubborn man. The hours passed.
We've tried Spanish, French, Italian, Greek, Hebrew . . .
Perhaps some combination of letters . . .
No dinner, no breakfast . . . they'll starve!

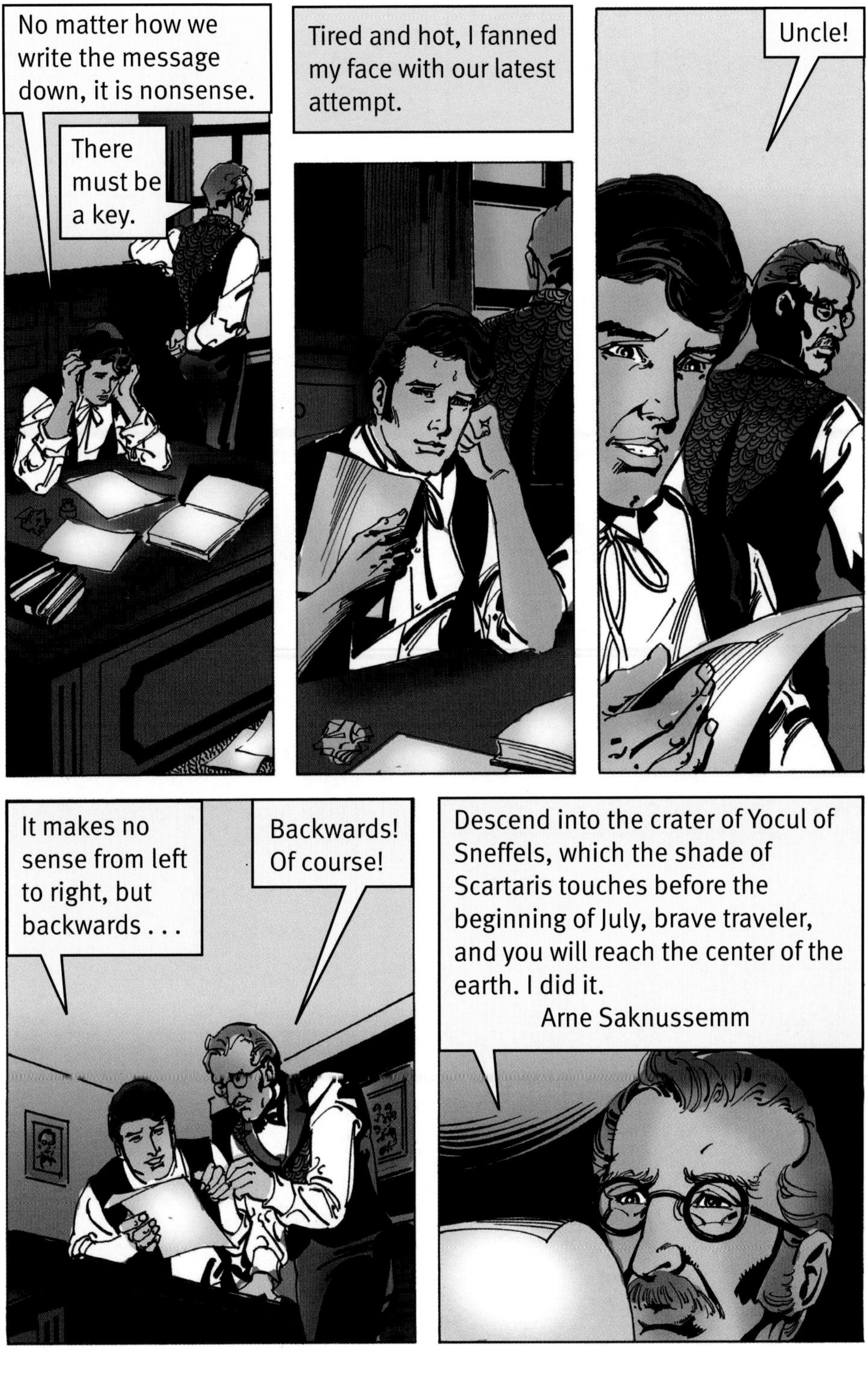
No matter how we write the message down, it is nonsense.
There must be a key.
Tired and hot, I fanned my face with our latest attempt.
Uncle!
It makes no sense from left to right, but backwards . . .
Backwards! Of course!
Descend into the crater of Yocul of Sneffels, which the shade of Scartaris touches before the beginning of July, brave traveler, and you will reach the center of the earth. I did it.
Arne Saknussemm

But what does it mean? What are Sneffels and Scartaris?

Sneffels is an extinct volcano in Iceland. Scartaris is the name of one of its peaks.

Before the beginning of July, Scartaris must cast its shadow over the opening of the one crater that led to the center of the earth.

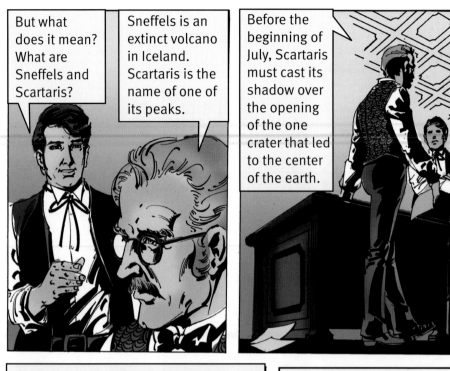

But scientists believe that the deeper you go into the earth, the hotter it becomes. At the center it must be twenty thousand degrees!

I do not believe in the dangers and difficulties! The only way to learn is, like Arne Saknussemm, to go and see!

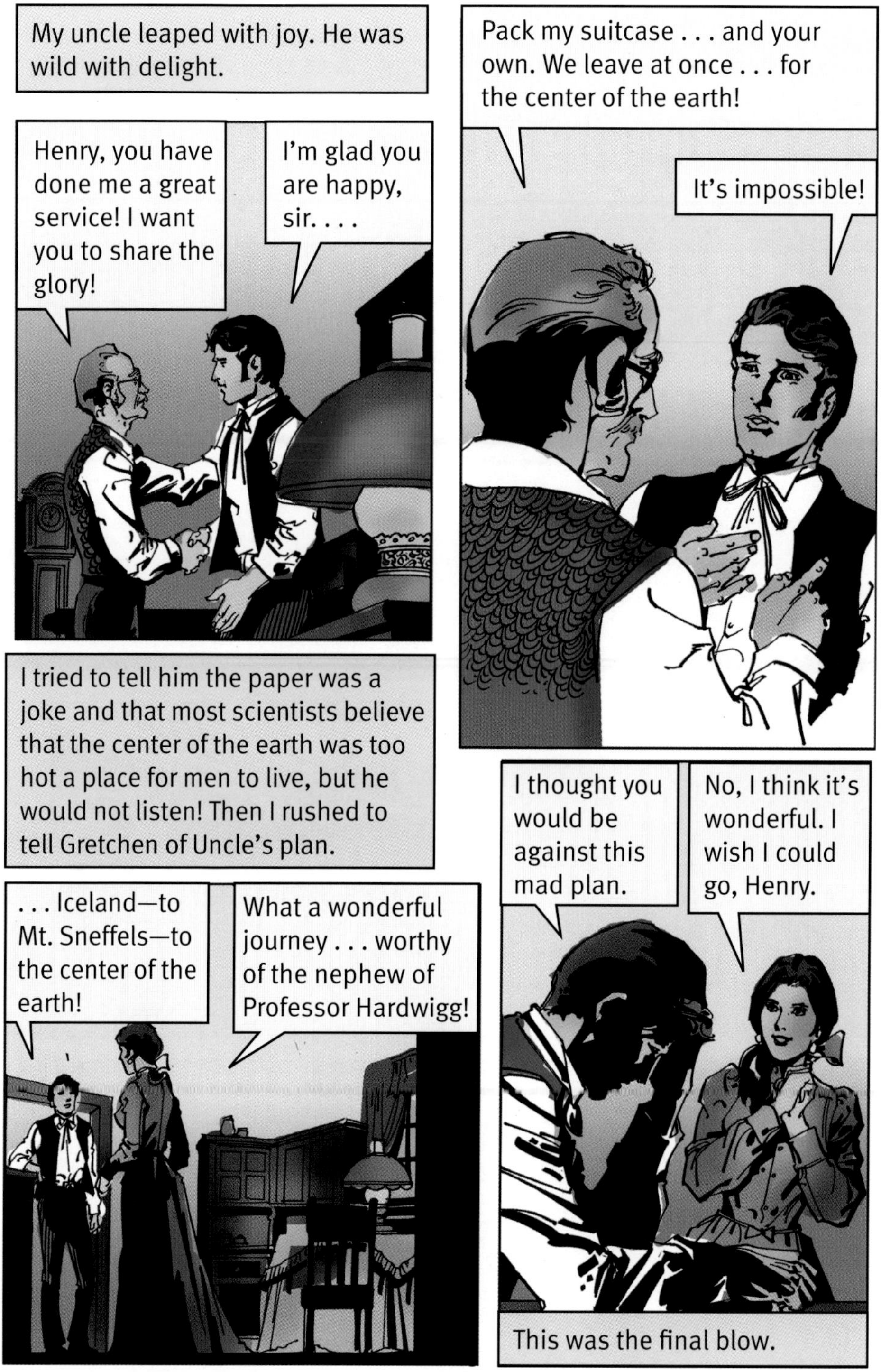
My uncle leaped with joy. He was wild with delight.
Henry, you have done me a great service! I want you to share the glory!
I'm glad you are happy, sir. . . .
Pack my suitcase . . . and your own. We leave at once . . . for the center of the earth!
It's impossible!
I tried to tell him the paper was a joke and that most scientists believe that the center of the earth was too hot a place for men to live, but he would not listen! Then I rushed to tell Gretchen of Uncle's plan.
. . . Iceland—to Mt. Sneffels—to the center of the earth!
What a wonderful journey . . . worthy of the nephew of Professor Hardwigg!
I thought you would be against this mad plan.
No, I think it's wonderful. I wish I could go, Henry.
This was the final blow.

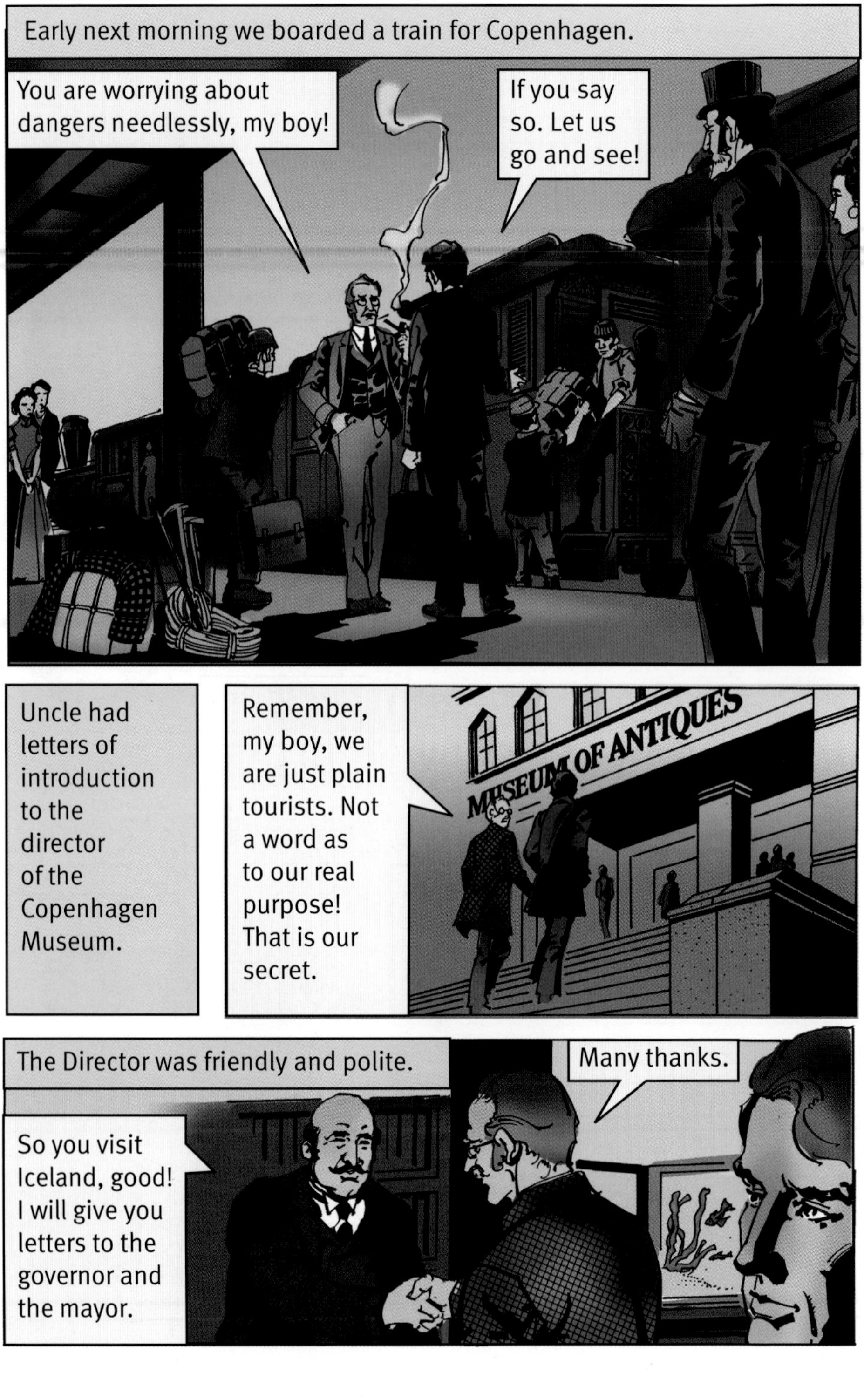
Early next morning we boarded a train for Copenhagen.
You are worrying about dangers needlessly, my boy!
If you say so. Let us go and see!
Uncle had letters of introduction to the director of the Copenhagen Museum.
Remember, my boy, we are just plain tourists. Not a word as to our real purpose! That is our secret.
MUSEUM OF ANTIQUES
The Director was friendly and polite.
So you visit Iceland, good! I will give you letters to the governor and the mayor.
Many thanks.

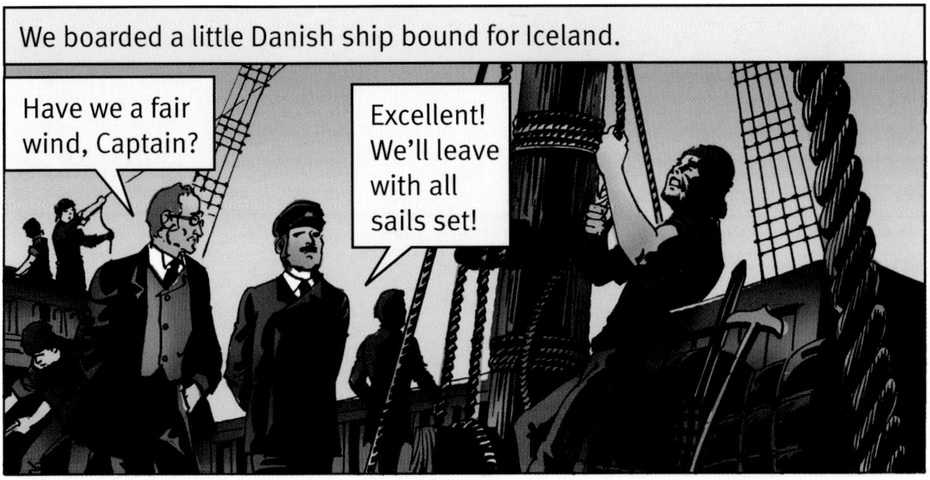
We boarded a little Danish ship bound for Iceland.
Have we a fair wind, Captain?
Excellent! We'll leave with all sails set!

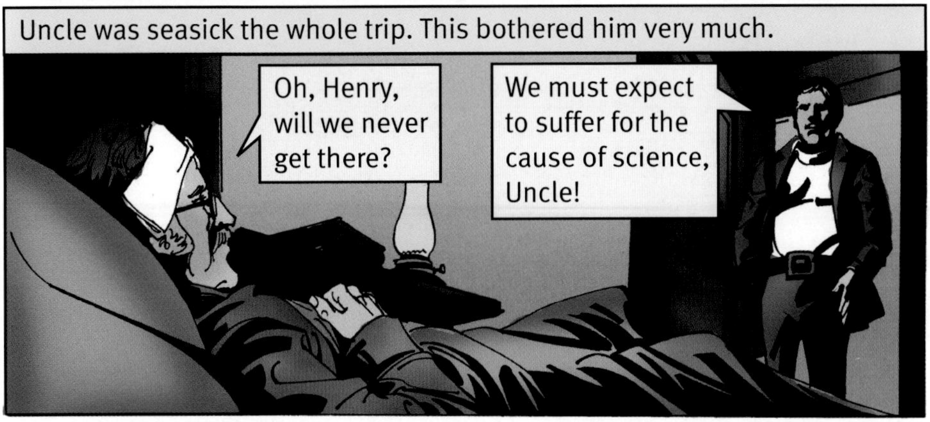
Uncle was seasick the whole trip. This bothered him very much.
Oh, Henry, will we never get there?
We must expect to suffer for the cause of science, Uncle!

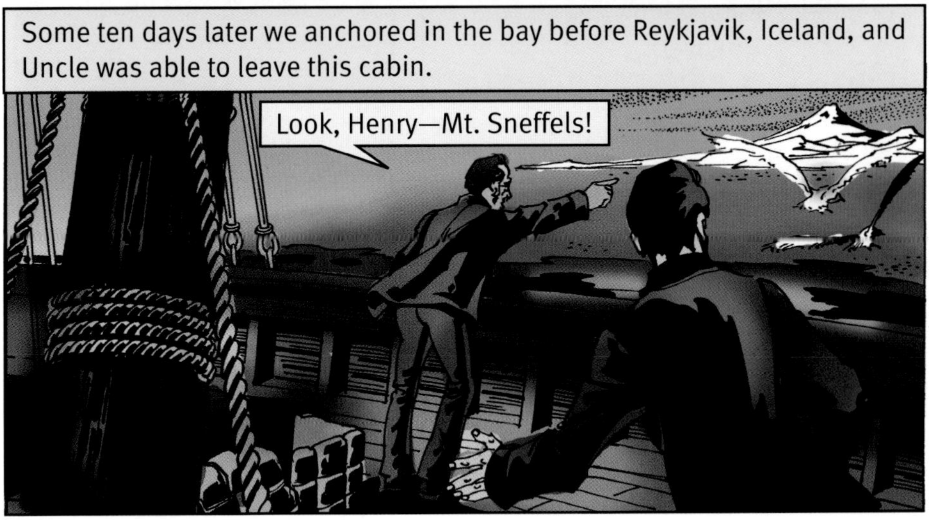
Some ten days later we anchored in the bay before Reykjavik, Iceland, and Uncle was able to leave this cabin.
Look, Henry—Mt. Sneffels!

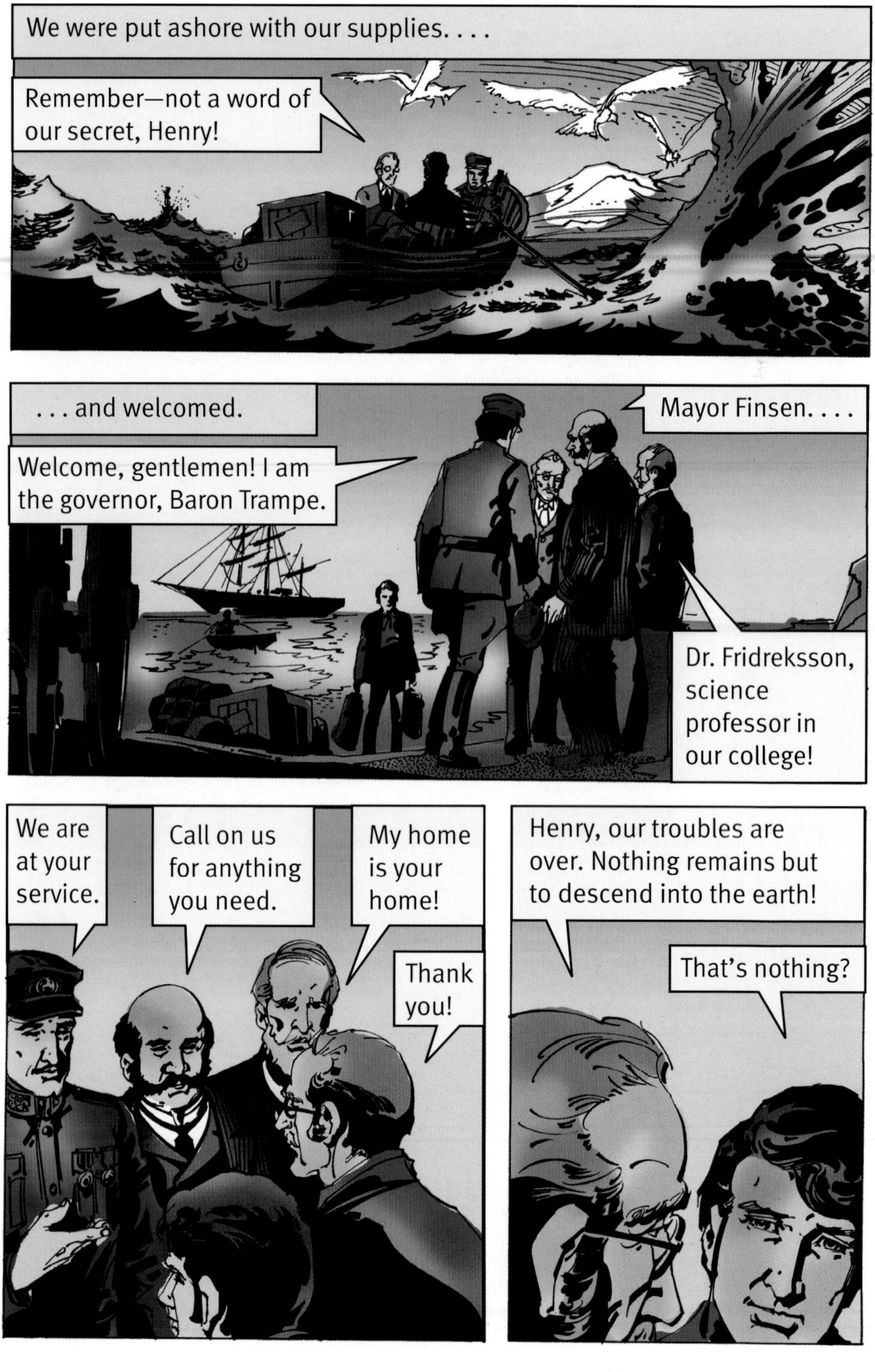
We were put ashore with our supplies. . . .
Remember—not a word of our secret, Henry!
. . . and welcomed.
Welcome, gentlemen! I am the governor, Baron Trampe.
Mayor Finsen. . . .
Dr. Fridreksson, science professor in our college!
We are at your service.
Call on us for anything you need.
My home is your home!
Thank you!
Henry, our troubles are over. Nothing remains but to descend into the earth!
That's nothing?

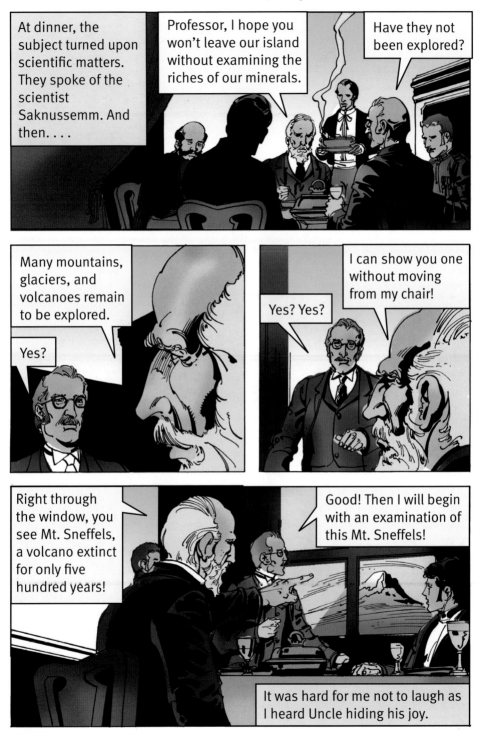

At dinner, the subject turned upon scientific matters. They spoke of the scientist Saknussemm. And then. . . .

Professor, I hope you won't leave our island without examining the riches of our minerals.

Have they not been explored?

Many mountains, glaciers, and volcanoes remain to be explored.

Yes?

Yes? Yes?

I can show you one without moving from my chair!

Right through the window, you see Mt. Sneffels, a volcano extinct for only five hundred years!

Good! Then I will begin with an examination of this Mt. Sneffels!

It was hard for me not to laugh as I heard Uncle hiding his joy.

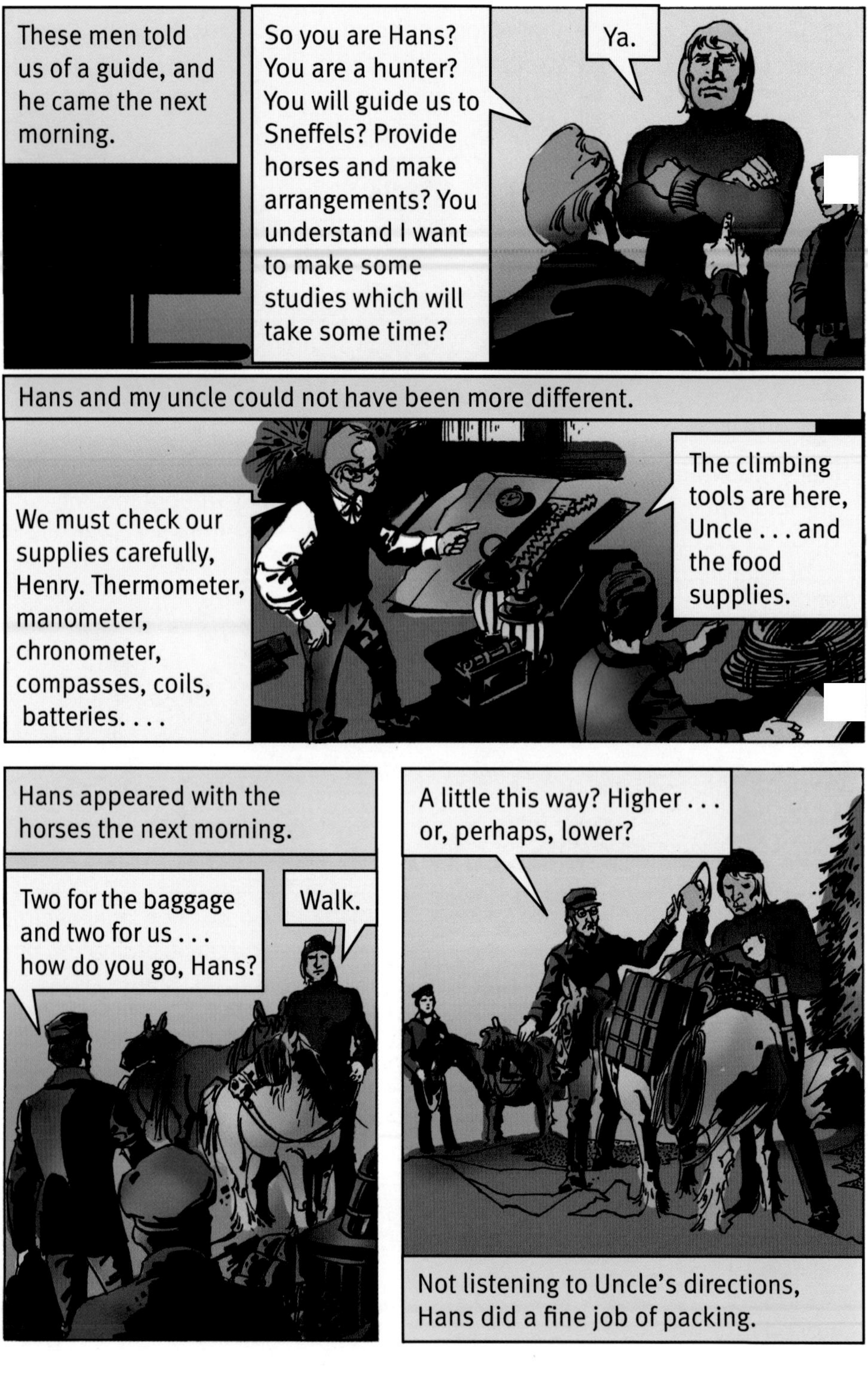
These men told us of a guide, and he came the next morning.
So you are Hans? You are a hunter? You will guide us to Sneffels? Provide horses and make arrangements? You understand I want to make some studies which will take some time?
Ya.
Hans and my uncle could not have been more different.
We must check our supplies carefully, Henry. Thermometer, manometer, chronometer, compasses, coils, batteries. . . .
The climbing tools are here, Uncle . . . and the food supplies.
Hans appeared with the horses the next morning.
Two for the baggage and two for us . . . how do you go, Hans?
Walk.
A little this way? Higher . . . or, perhaps, lower?
Not listening to Uncle's directions, Hans did a fine job of packing.

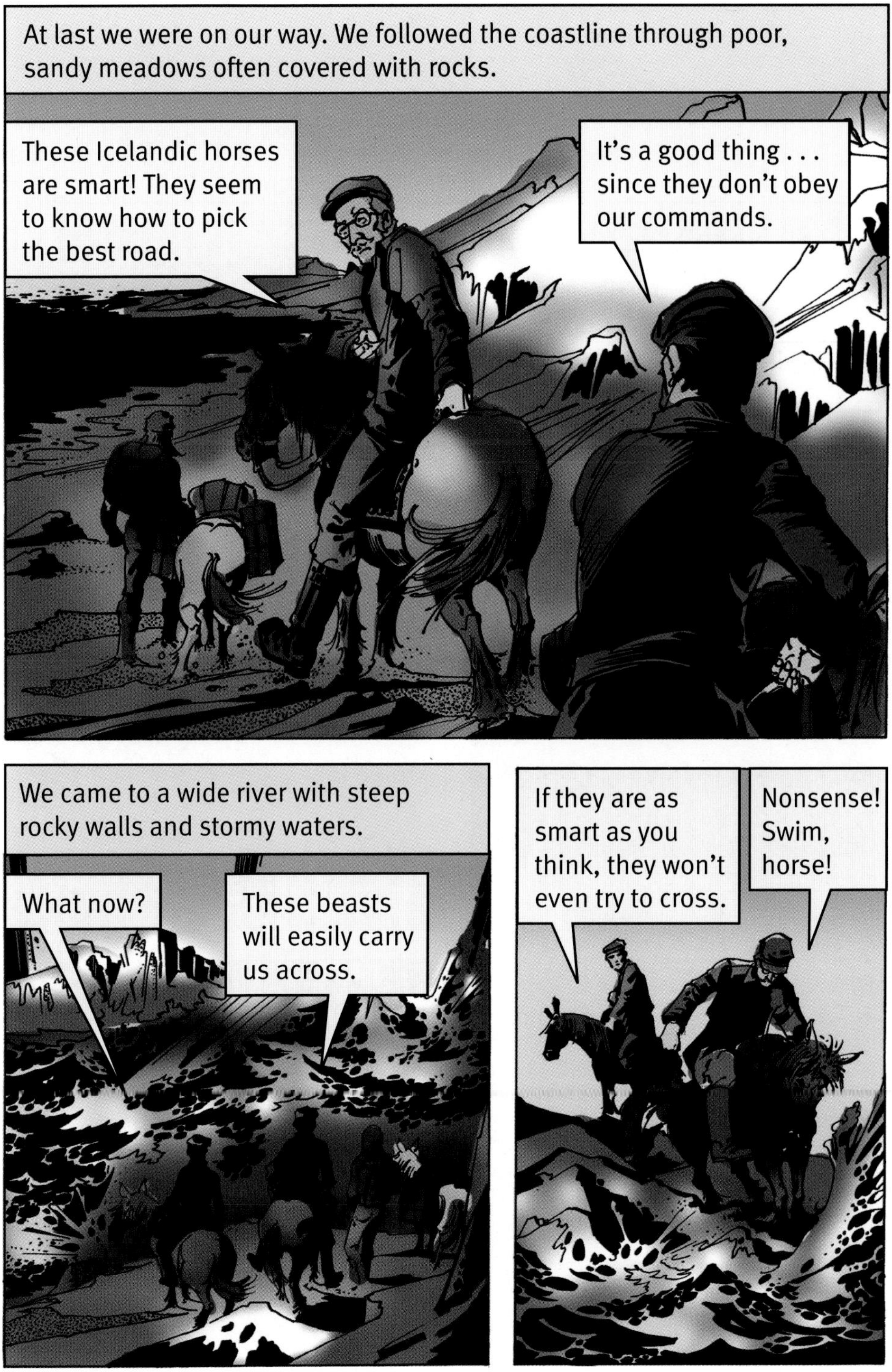
At last we were on our way. We followed the coastline through poor, sandy meadows often covered with rocks.
These Icelandic horses are smart! They seem to know how to pick the best road.
It's a good thing . . . since they don't obey our commands.
We came to a wide river with steep rocky walls and stormy waters.
What now?
These beasts will easily carry us across.
If they are as smart as you think, they won't even try to cross.
Nonsense! Swim, horse!

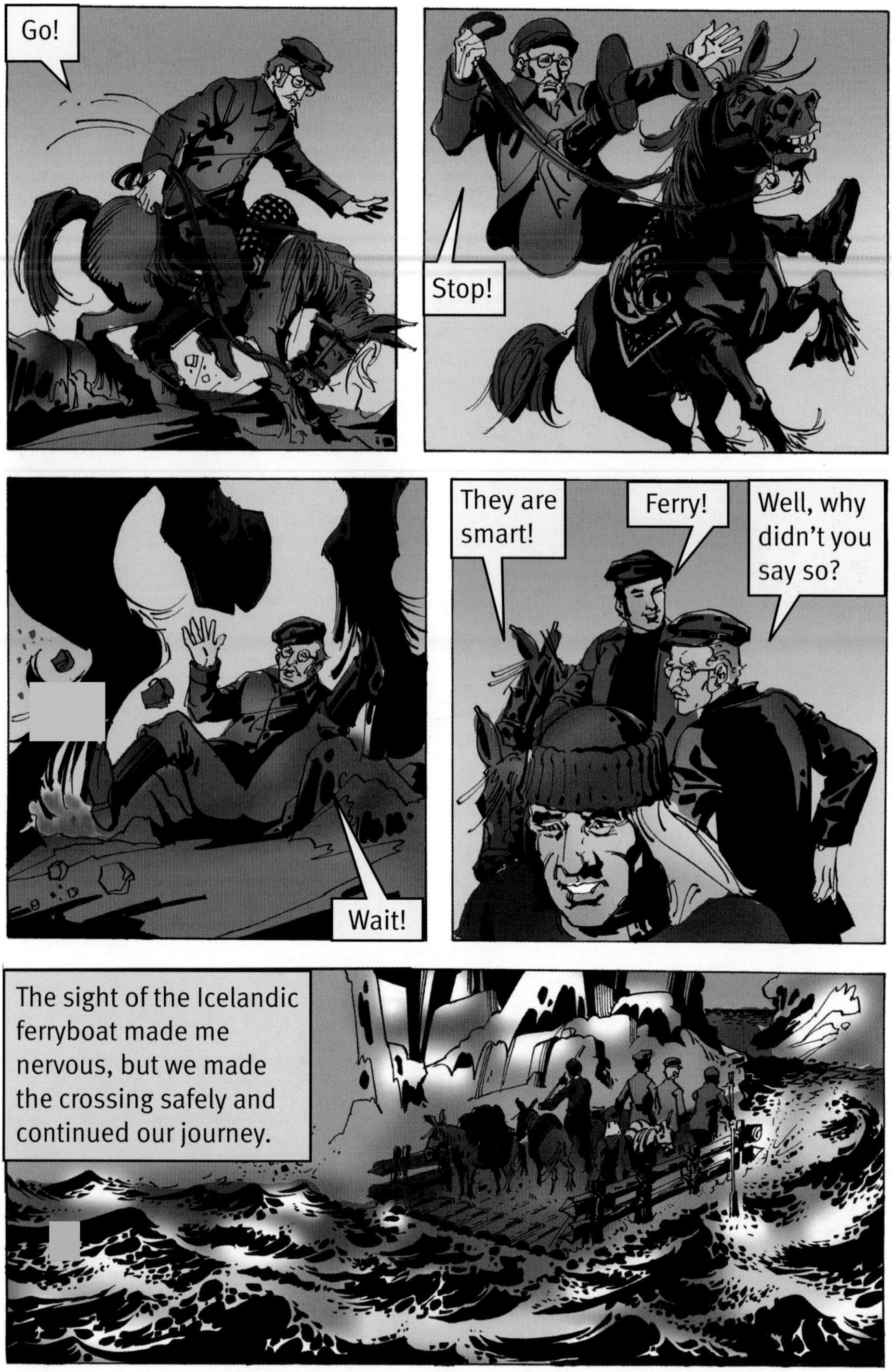
Go!
Stop!
Wait!
They are smart!
Ferry!
Well, why didn't you say so?
The sight of the Icelandic ferryboat made me nervous, but we made the crossing safely and continued our journey.

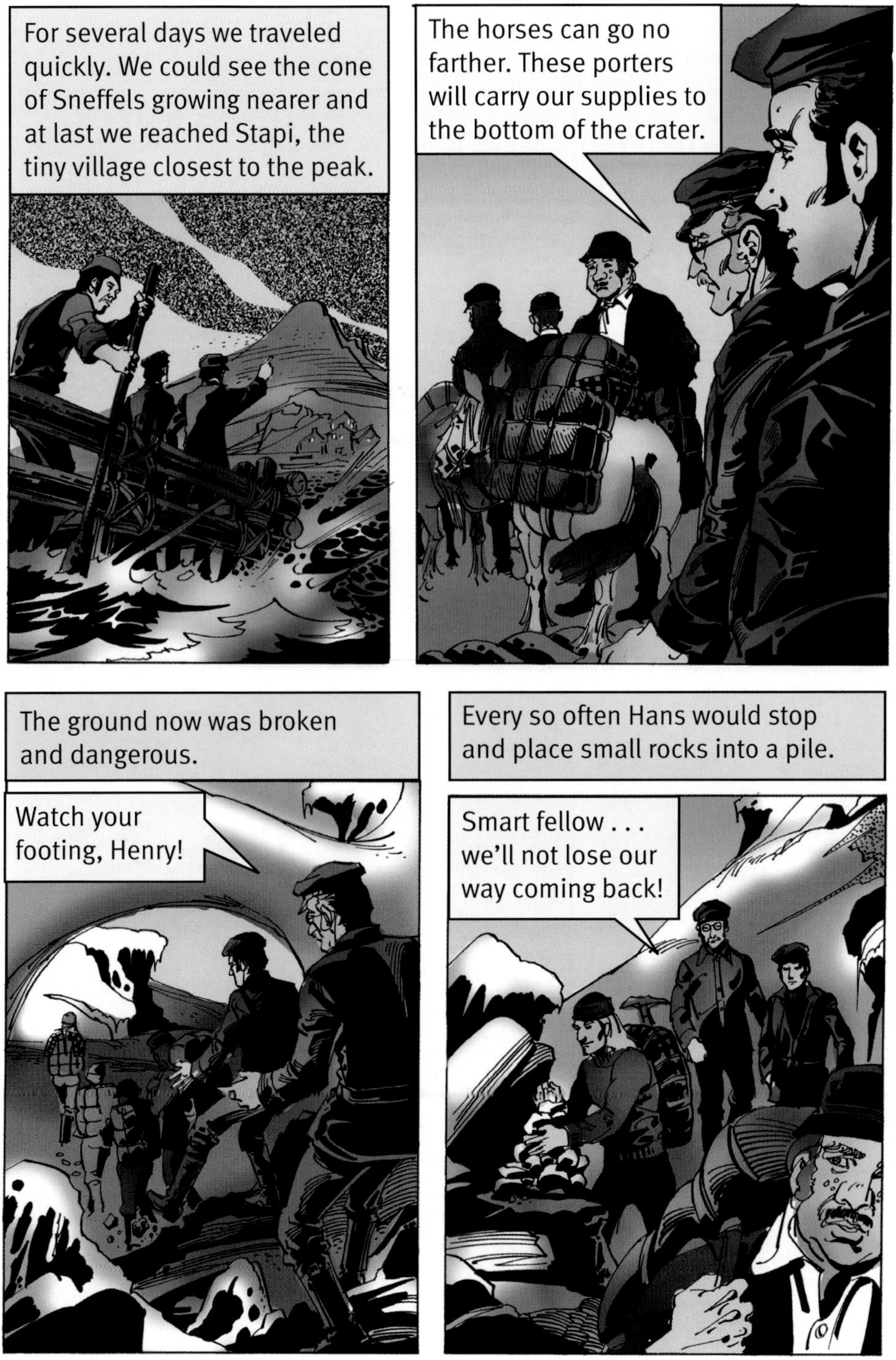
For several days we traveled quickly. We could see the cone of Sneffels growing nearer and at last we reached Stapi, the tiny village closest to the peak.
The horses can go no farther. These porters will carry our supplies to the bottom of the crater.
The ground now was broken and dangerous.
Watch your footing, Henry!
Every so often Hans would stop and place small rocks into a pile.
Smart fellow . . . we'll not lose our way coming back!

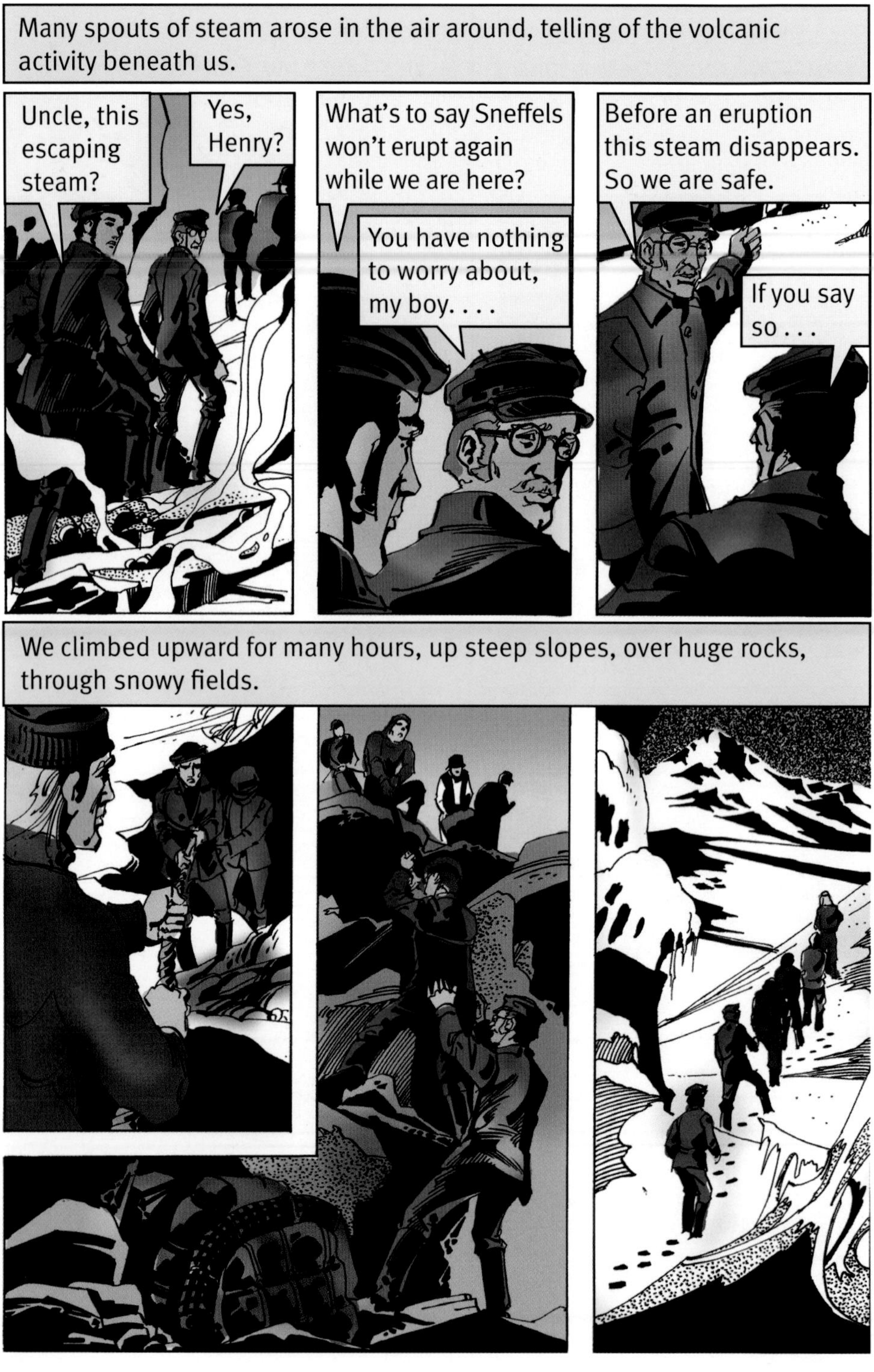
Many spouts of steam arose in the air around, telling of the volcanic activity beneath us.
Uncle, this escaping steam?
Yes, Henry?
What's to say Sneffels won't erupt again while we are here?
You have nothing to worry about, my boy. . . .
Before an eruption this steam disappears. So we are safe.
If you say so . . .
We climbed upward for many hours, up steep slopes, over huge rocks, through snowy fields.

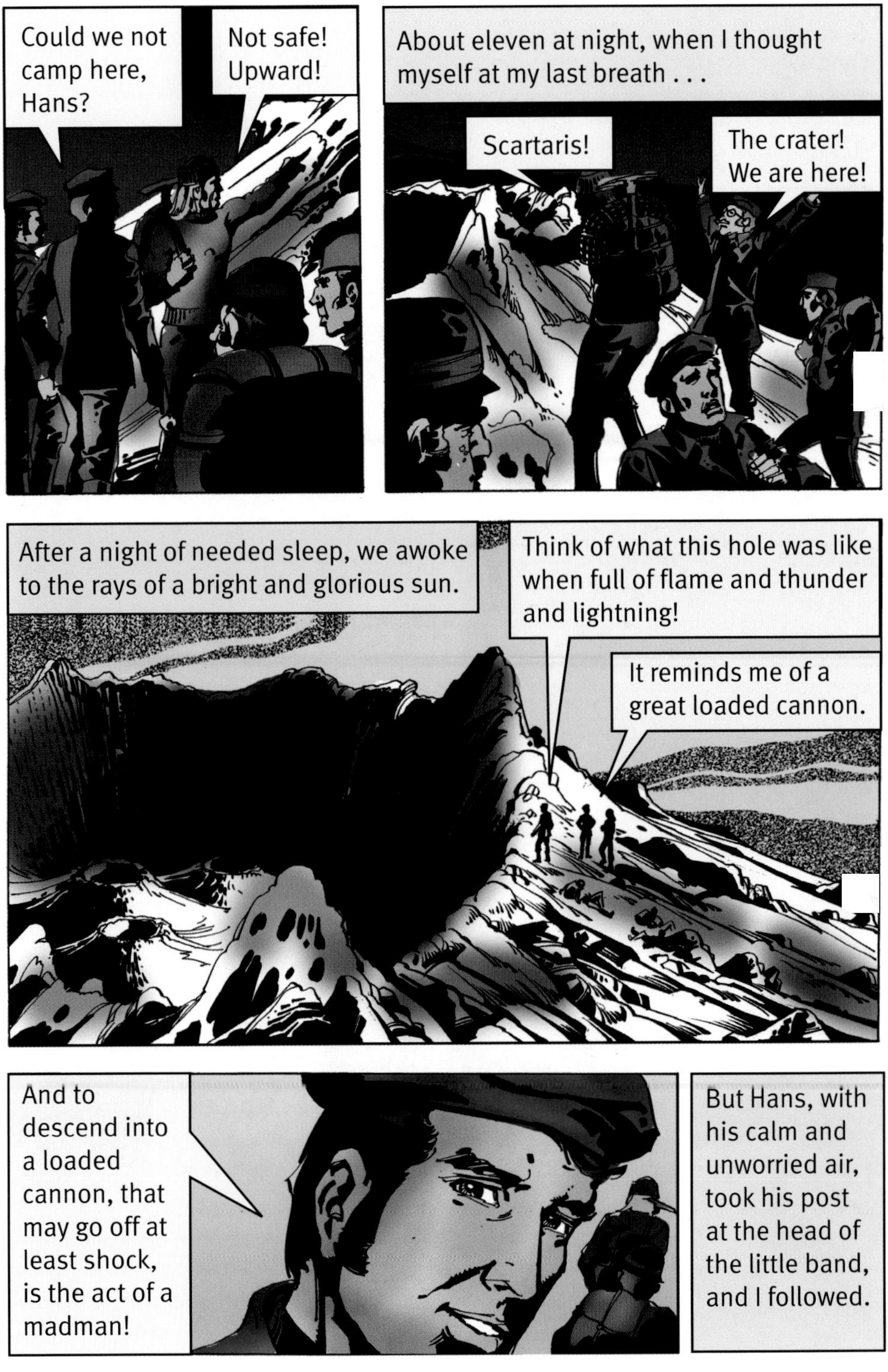
Could we not camp here, Hans?
Not safe! Upward!
About eleven at night, when I thought myself at my last breath . . .
Scartaris!
The crater! We are here!
After a night of needed sleep, we awoke to the rays of a bright and glorious sun.
Think of what this hole was like when full of flame and thunder and lightning!
It reminds me of a great loaded cannon.
And to descend into a loaded cannon, that may go off at least shock, is the act of a madman!
But Hans, with his calm and unworried air, took his post at the head of the little band, and I followed.

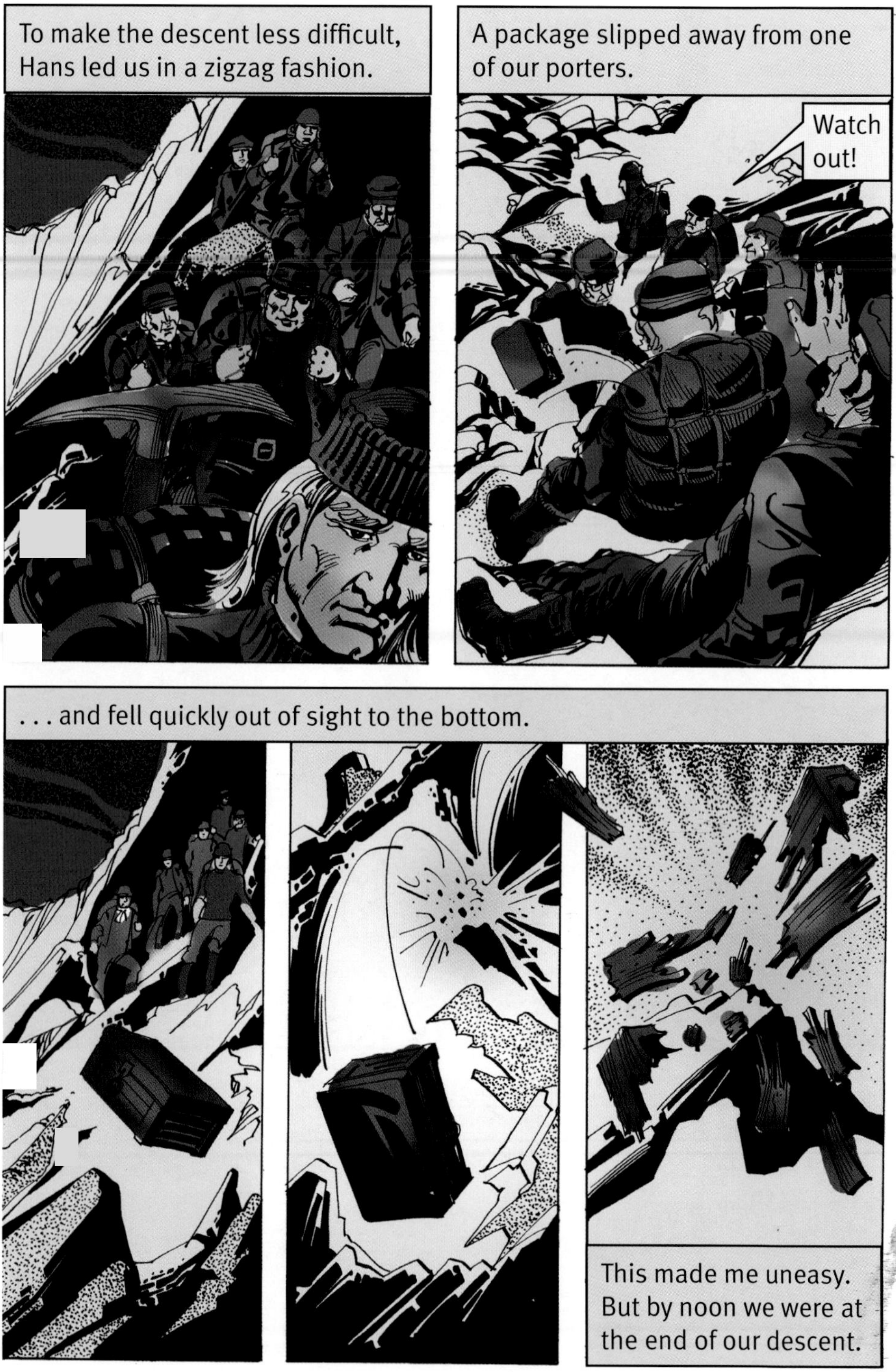
To make the descent less difficult, Hans led us in a zigzag fashion.
A package slipped away from one of our porters.
Watch out!
. . . and fell quickly out of sight to the bottom.
This made me uneasy. But by noon we were at the end of our descent.

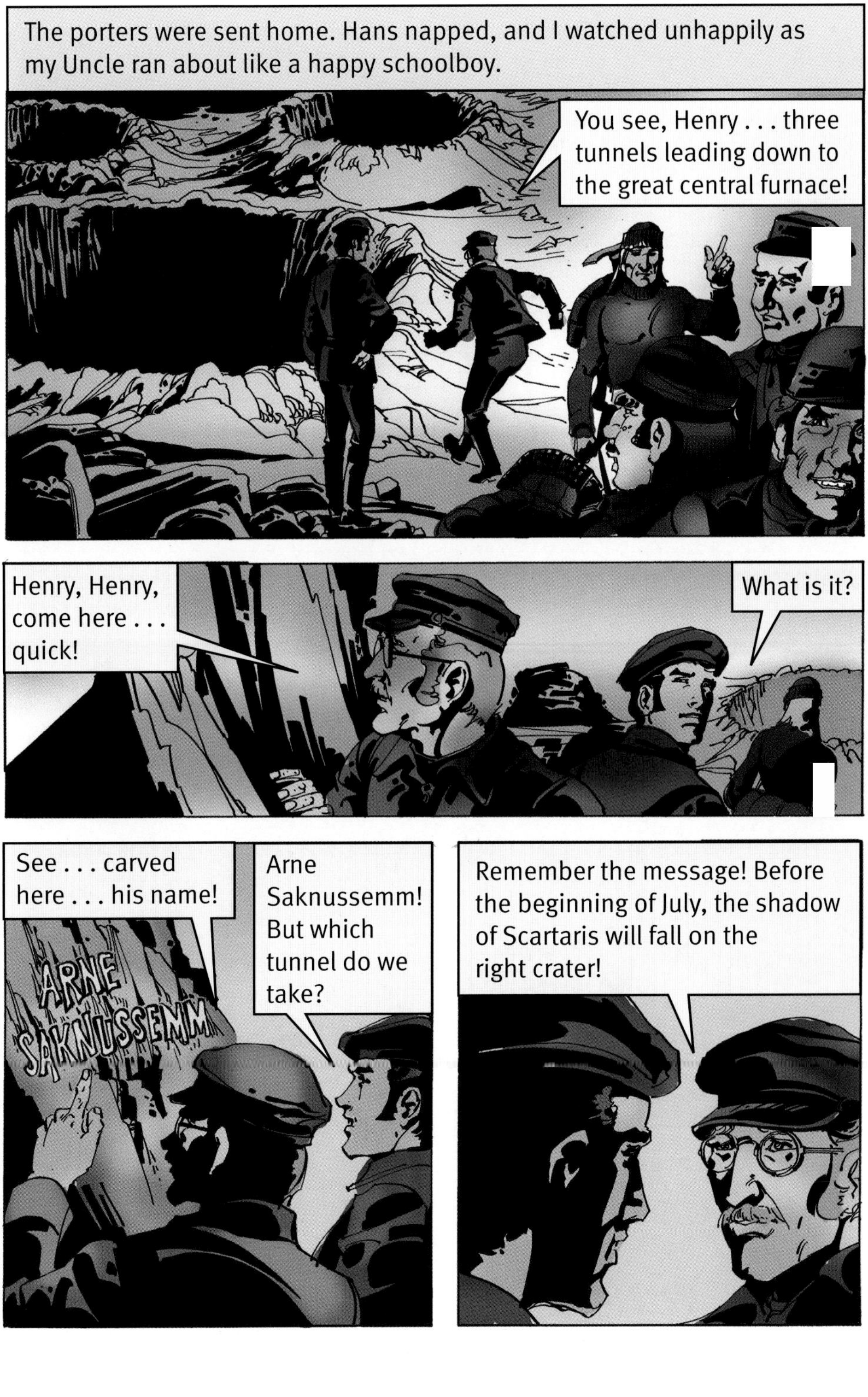
The porters were sent home. Hans napped, and I watched unhappily as my Uncle ran about like a happy schoolboy.
You see, Henry . . . three tunnels leading down to the great central furnace!
Henry, Henry, come here . . . quick!
What is it?
See . . . carved here . . . his name!
ARNE SAKNUSSEMM
Arne Saknussemm! But which tunnel do we take?
Remember the message! Before the beginning of July, the shadow of Scartaris will fall on the right crater!

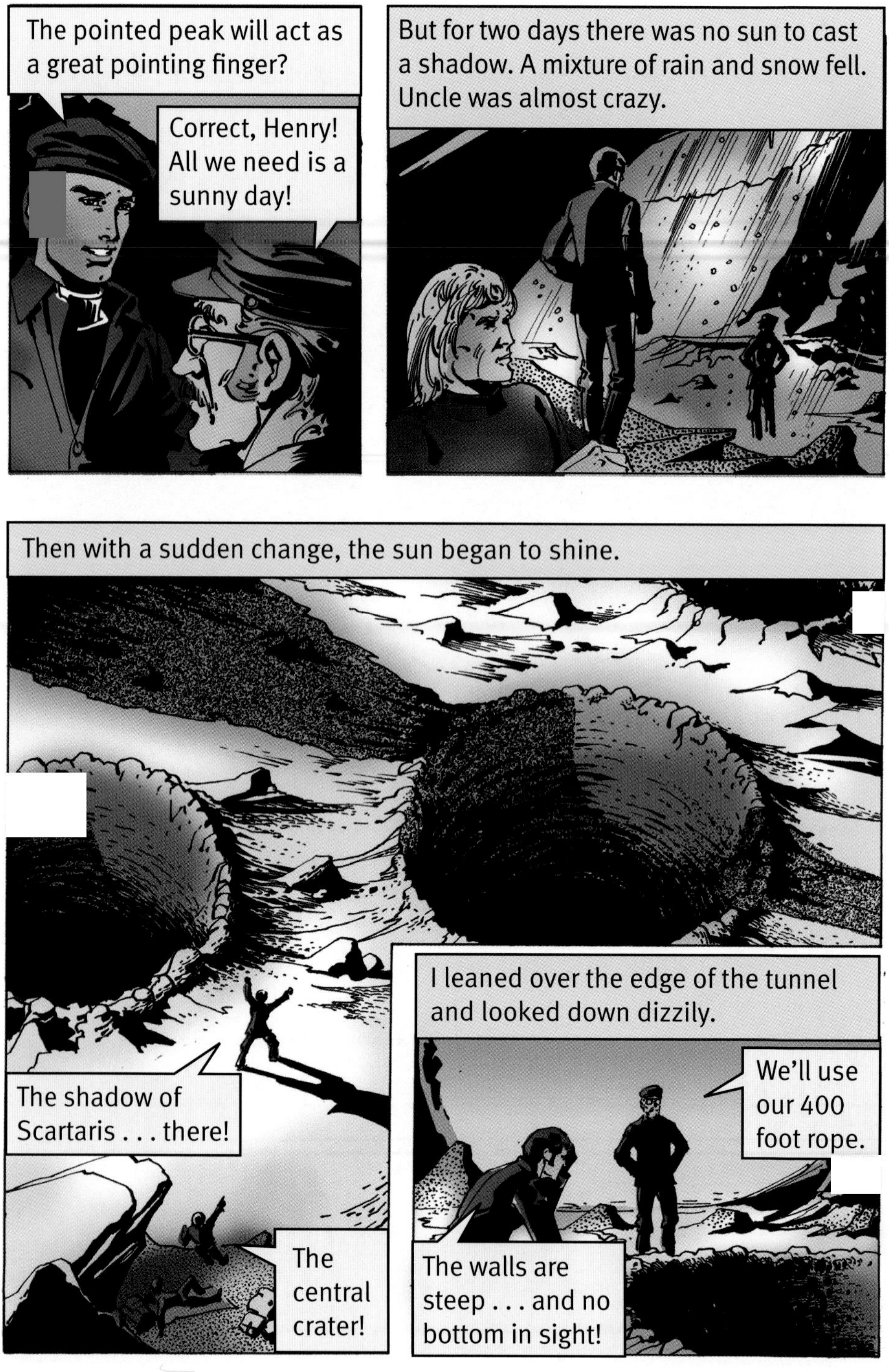
The pointed peak will act as a great pointing finger?
Correct, Henry! All we need is a sunny day!
But for two days there was no sun to cast a shadow. A mixture of rain and snow fell. Uncle was almost crazy.
Then with a sudden change, the sun began to shine.
The shadow of Scartaris . . . there!
The central crater!
I leaned over the edge of the tunnel and looked down dizzily.
We'll use our 400 foot rope.
The walls are steep . . . and no bottom in sight!

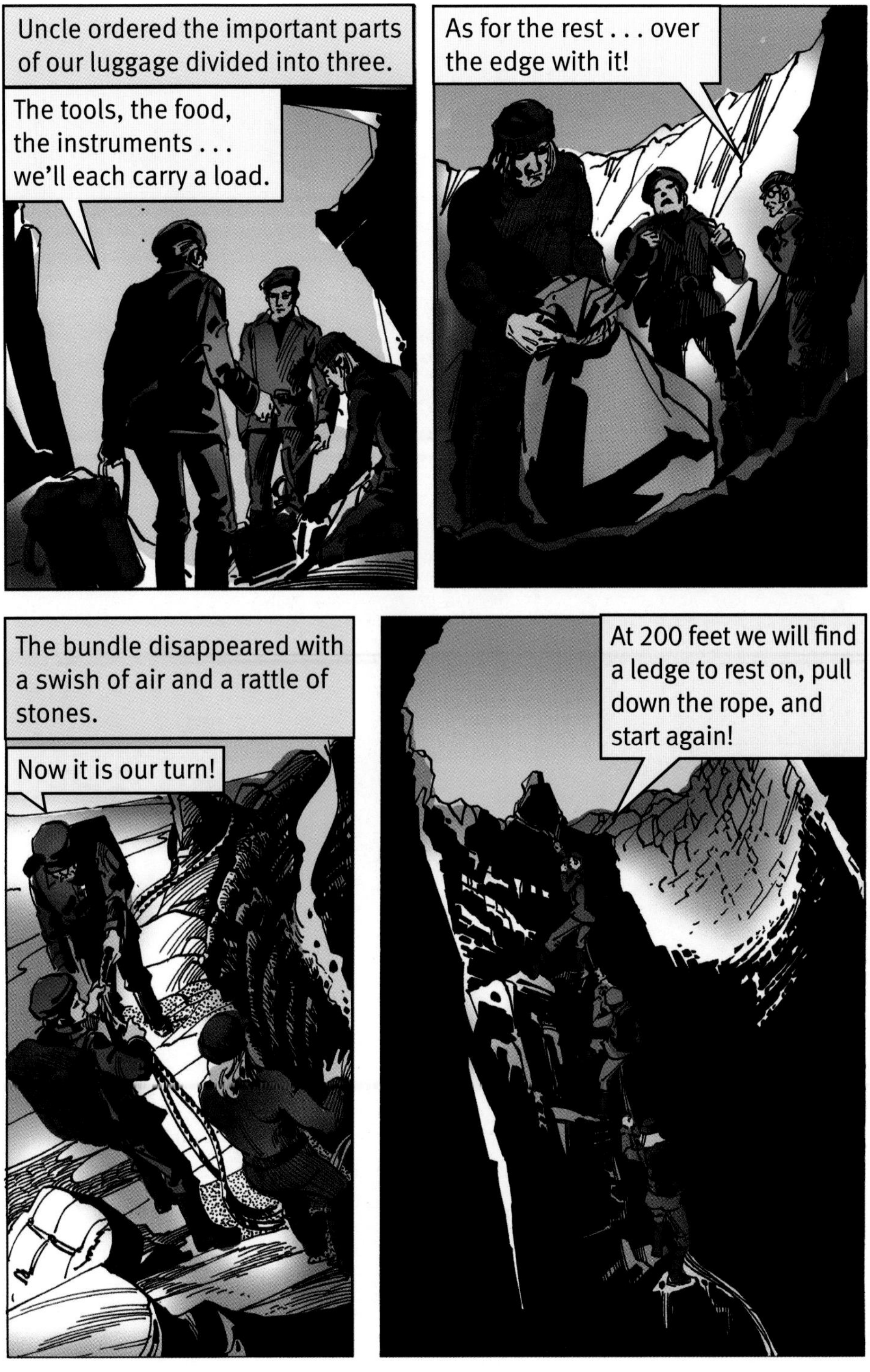
Uncle ordered the important parts of our luggage divided into three.
The tools, the food, the instruments . . . we'll each carry a load.
As for the rest . . . over the edge with it!
The bundle disappeared with a swish of air and a rattle of stones.
Now it is our turn!
At 200 feet we will find a ledge to rest on, pull down the rope, and start again!

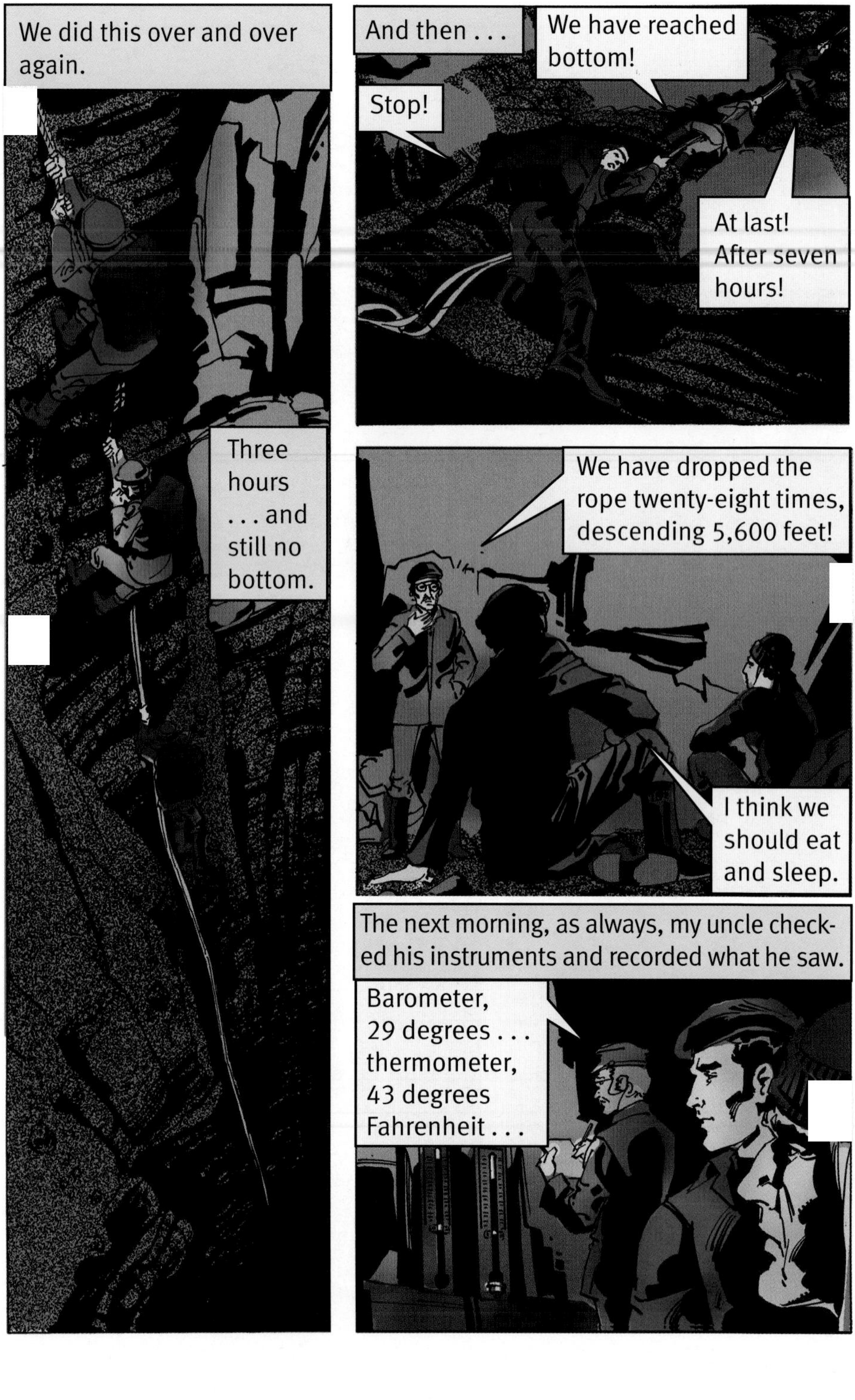
We did this over and over again.
Three hours . . . and still no bottom.
And then . . .
We have reached bottom!
Stop!
At last! After seven hours!
We have dropped the rope twenty-eight times, descending 5,600 feet!
I think we should eat and sleep.
The next morning, as always, my uncle checked his instruments and recorded what he saw.
Barometer, 29 degrees . . . thermometer, 43 degrees Fahrenheit . . .

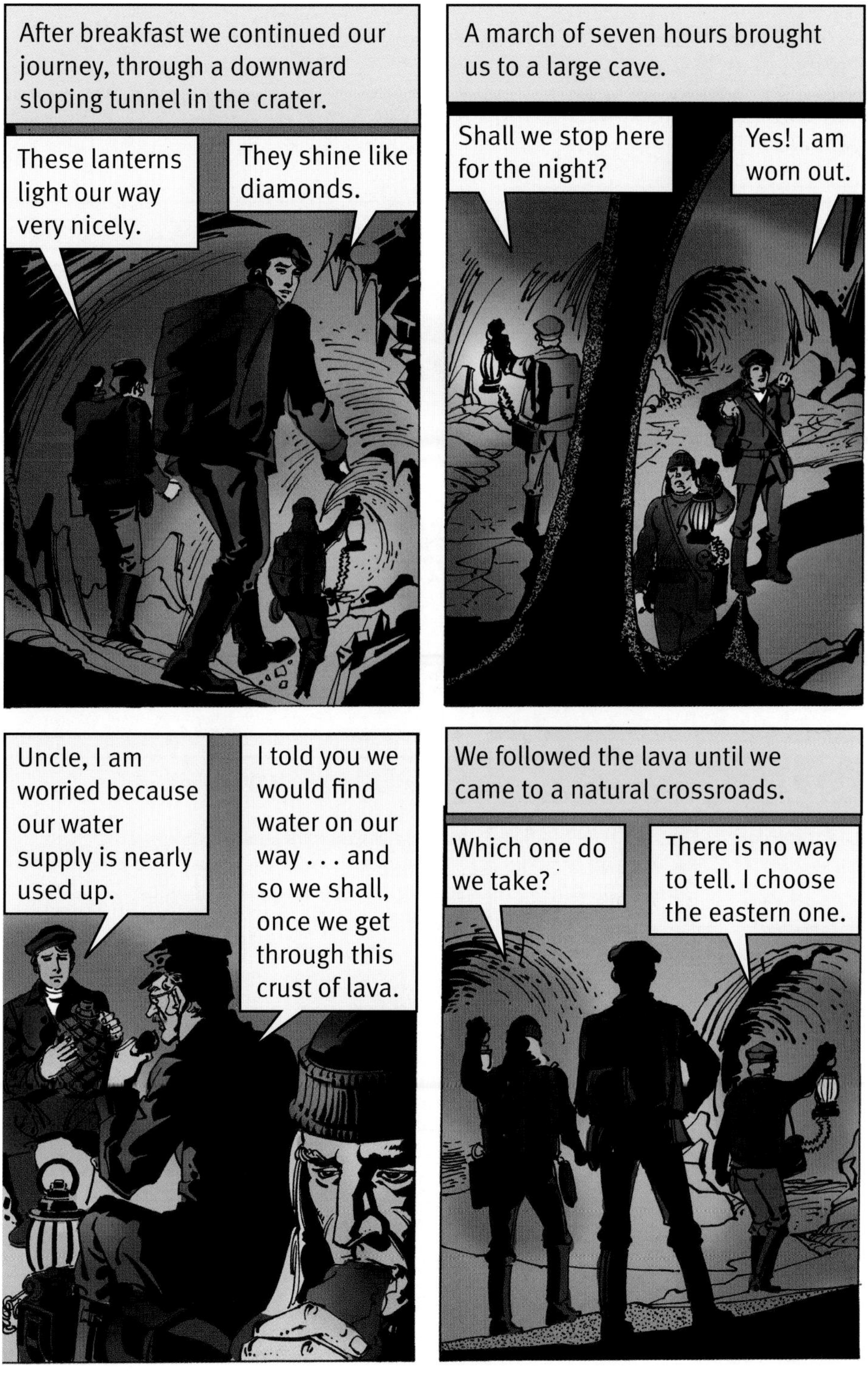
After breakfast we continued our journey, through a downward sloping tunnel in the crater.
These lanterns light our way very nicely.
They shine like diamonds.
A march of seven hours brought us to a large cave.
Shall we stop here for the night?
Yes! I am worn out.
Uncle, I am worried because our water supply is nearly used up.
I told you we would find water on our way . . . and so we shall, once we get through this crust of lava.
We followed the lava until we came to a natural crossroads.
Which one do we take?
There is no way to tell. I choose the eastern one.

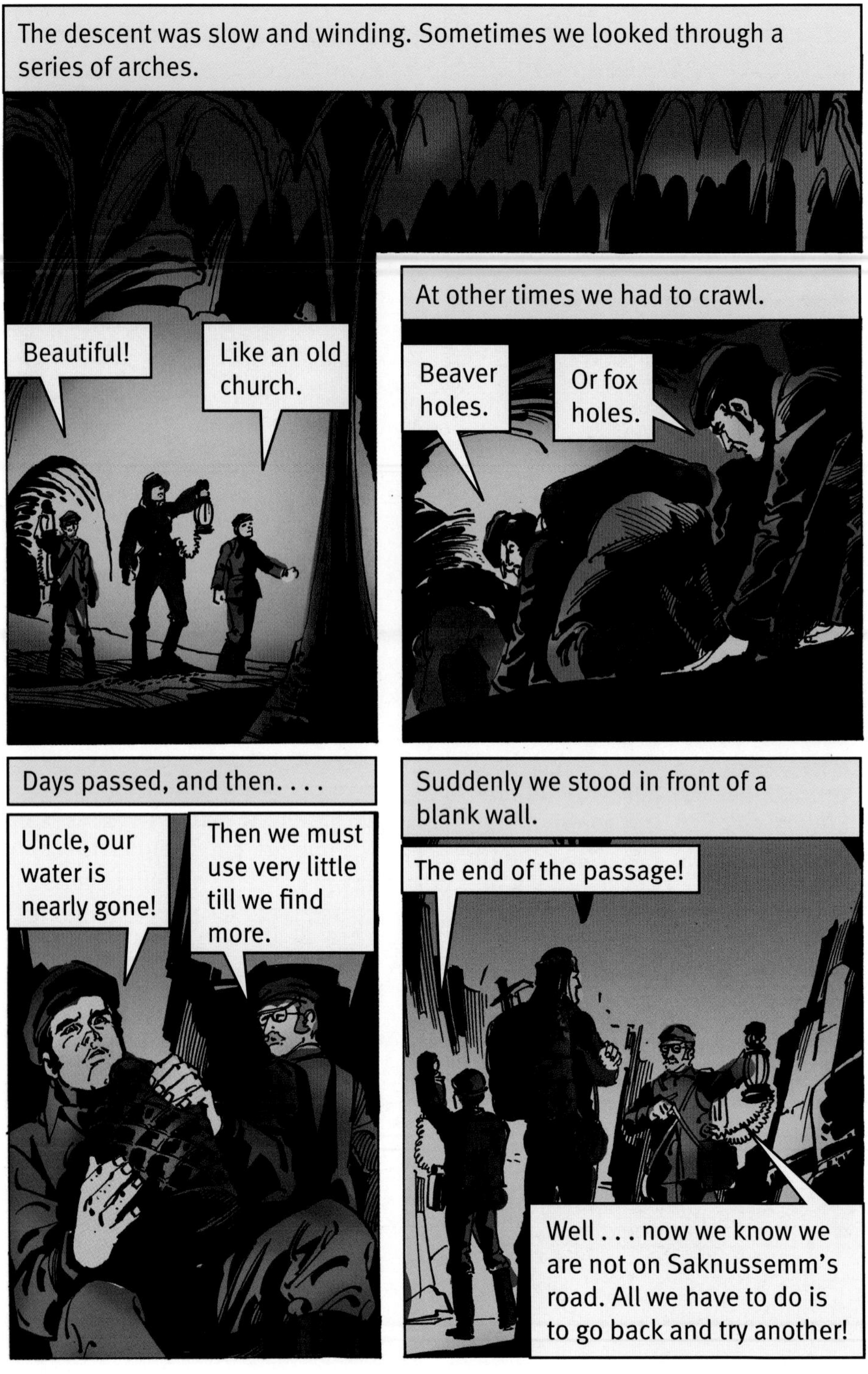
The descent was slow and winding. Sometimes we looked through a series of arches.
Beautiful!
Like an old church.
At other times we had to crawl.
Beaver holes.
Or fox holes.
Days passed, and then. . . .
Uncle, our water is nearly gone!
Then we must use very little till we find more.
Suddenly we stood in front of a blank wall.
The end of the passage!
Well . . . now we know we are not on Saknussemm's road. All we have to do is to go back and try another!

We'll take one night's rest, and in three days, I promise you, we shall be back to the crossroads.

But tomorrow there will not be a drop of water!

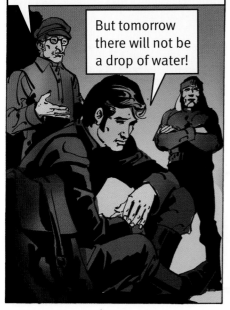

On the return trip we were hot and thirsty.

At last on the third day, after crawling on our hands and knees for hours...

The crossroads!

Thank heavens.

Presently, I felt my uncle near me. He lifted up my head.

Drink, my boy! The last mouthful . . . I saved it for you.

My dear uncle!

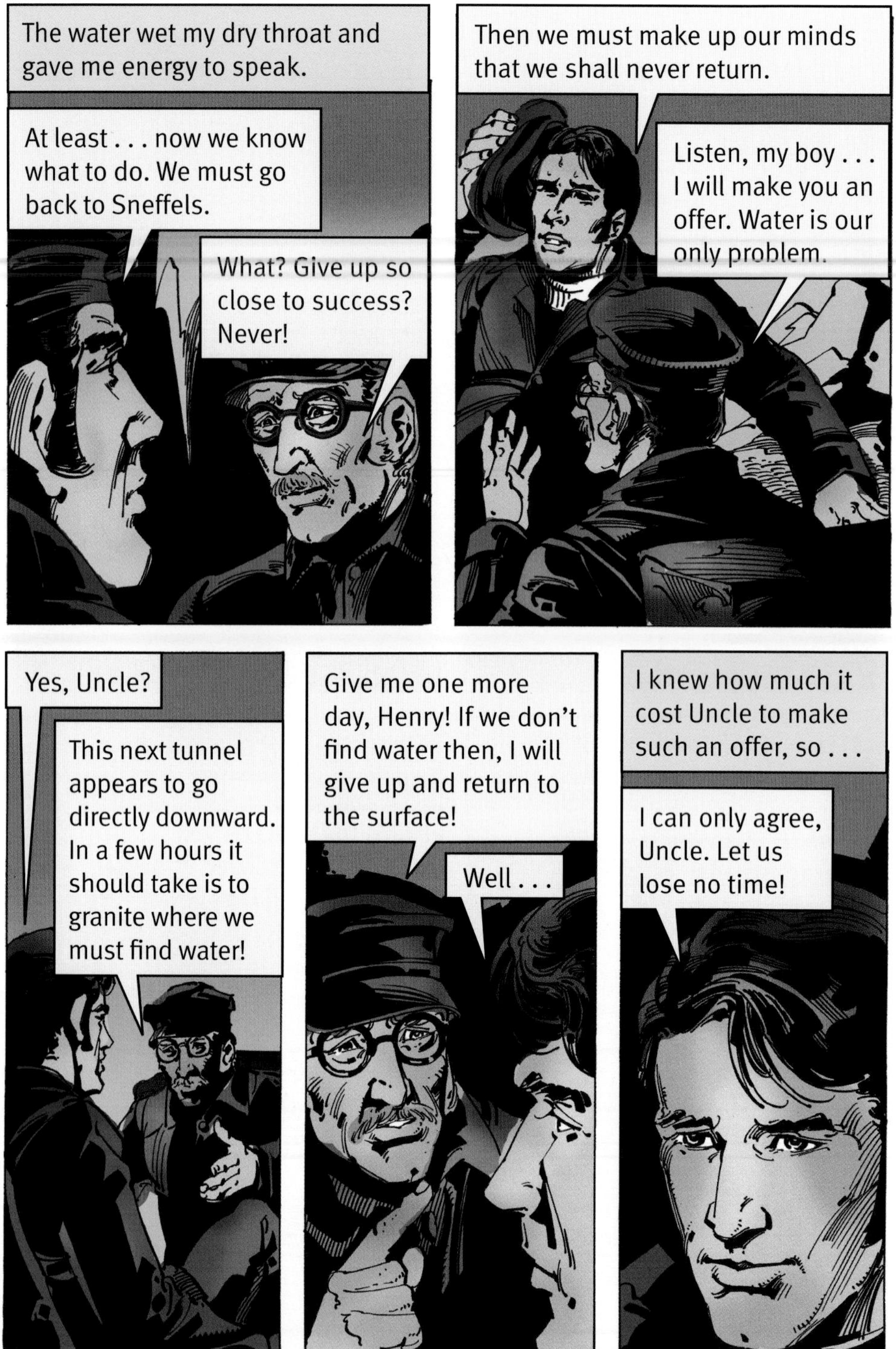
The water wet my dry throat and gave me energy to speak.
At least . . . now we know what to do. We must go back to Sneffels.
What? Give up so close to success? Never!
Then we must make up our minds that we shall never return.
Listen, my boy . . . I will make you an offer. Water is our only problem.
Yes, Uncle?
This next tunnel appears to go directly downward. In a few hours it should take is to granite where we must find water!
Give me one more day, Henry! If we don't find water then, I will give up and return to the surface!
Well . . .
I knew how much it cost Uncle to make such an offer, so . . .
I can only agree, Uncle. Let us lose no time!

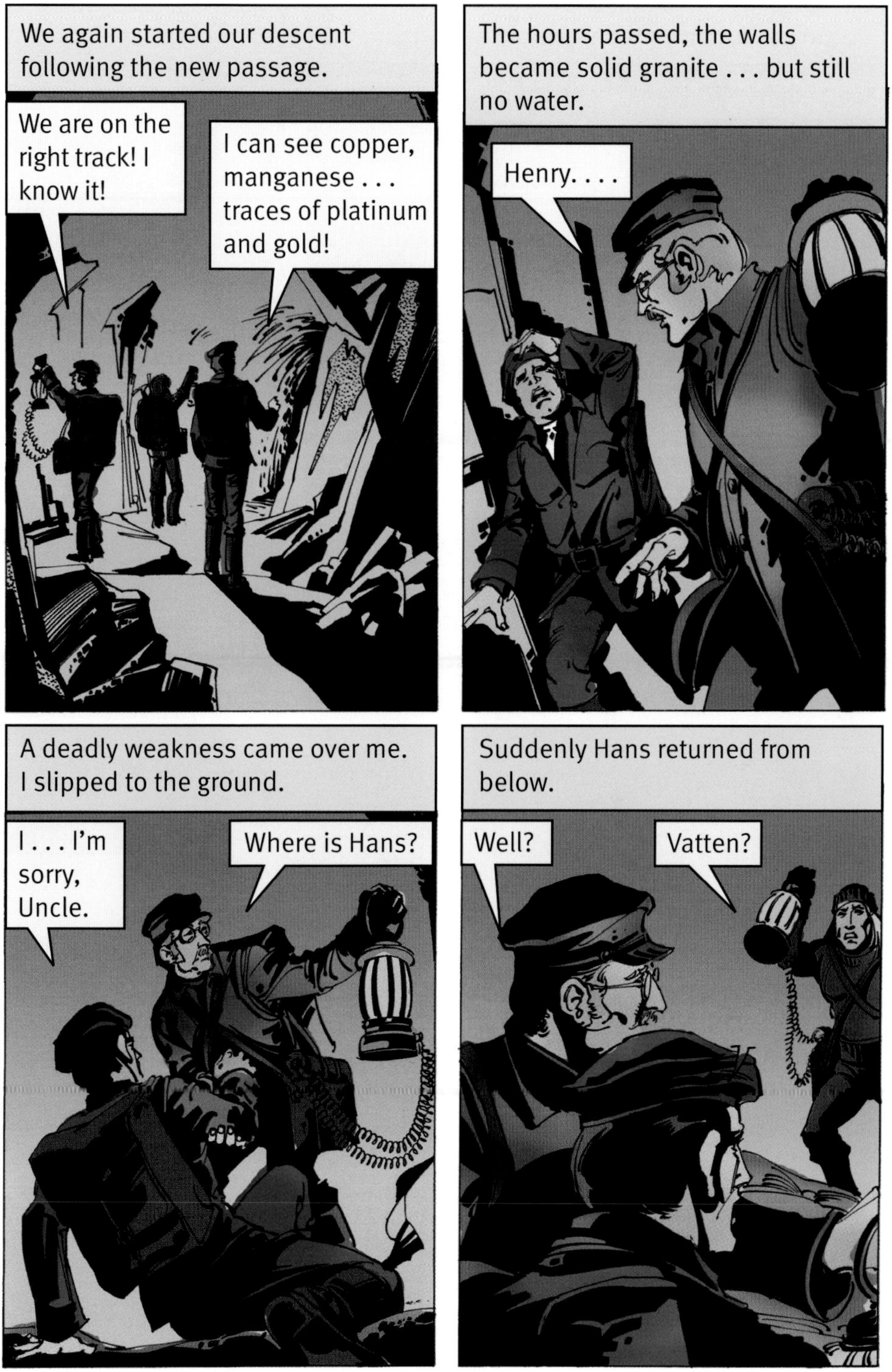
We again started our descent following the new passage.
We are on the right track! I know it!
I can see copper, manganese . . . traces of platinum and gold!
The hours passed, the walls became solid granite . . . but still no water.
Henry. . . .
A deadly weakness came over me. I slipped to the ground.
I . . . I'm sorry, Uncle.
Where is Hans?
Suddenly Hans returned from below.
Well?
Vatten?

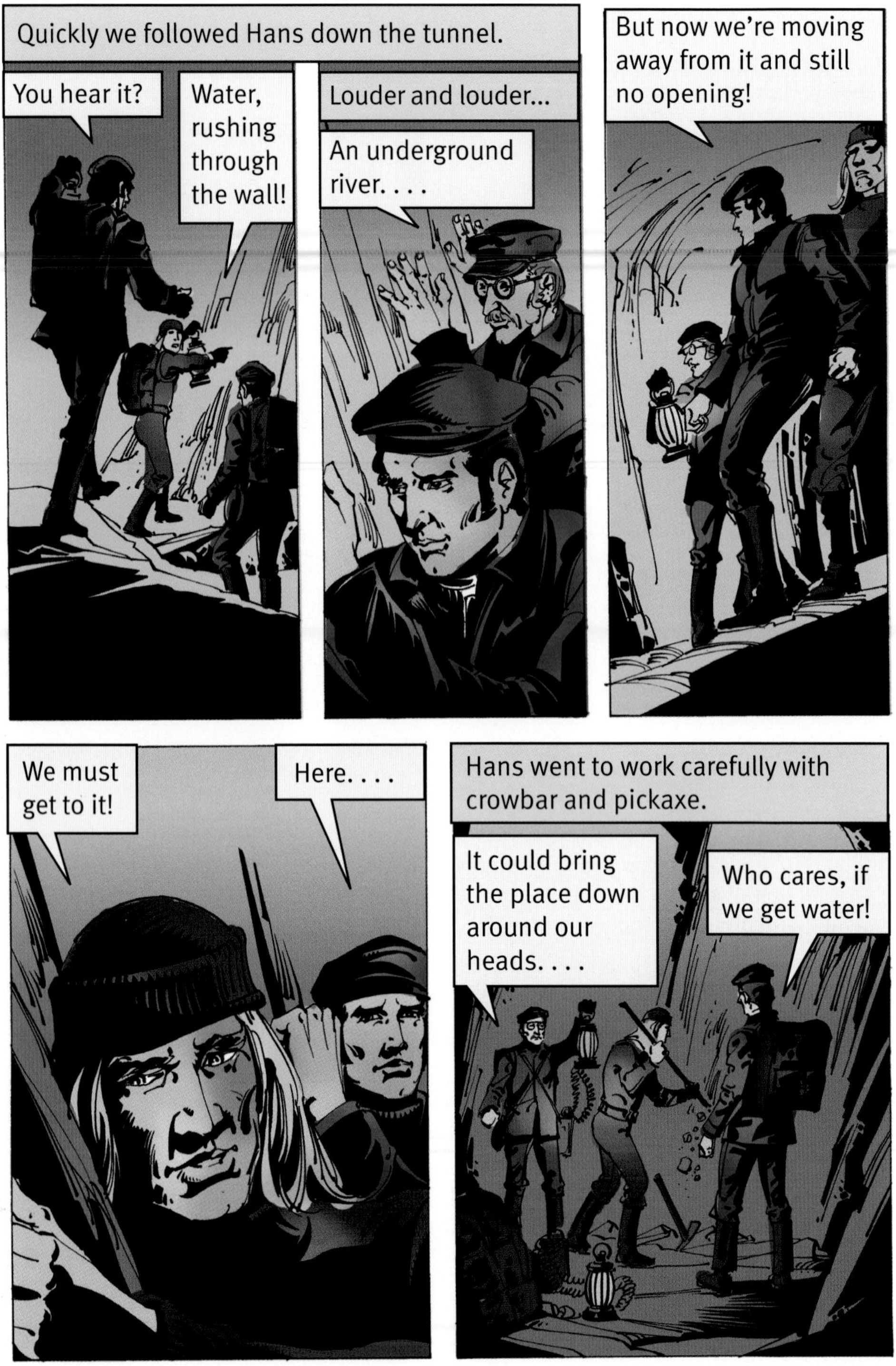
Quickly we followed Hans down the tunnel.
You hear it?
Water, rushing through the wall!
Louder and louder...
An underground river. . . .
But now we're moving away from it and still no opening!
We must get to it!
Here. . . .
Hans went to work carefully with crowbar and pickaxe.
It could bring the place down around our heads. . . .
Who cares, if we get water!

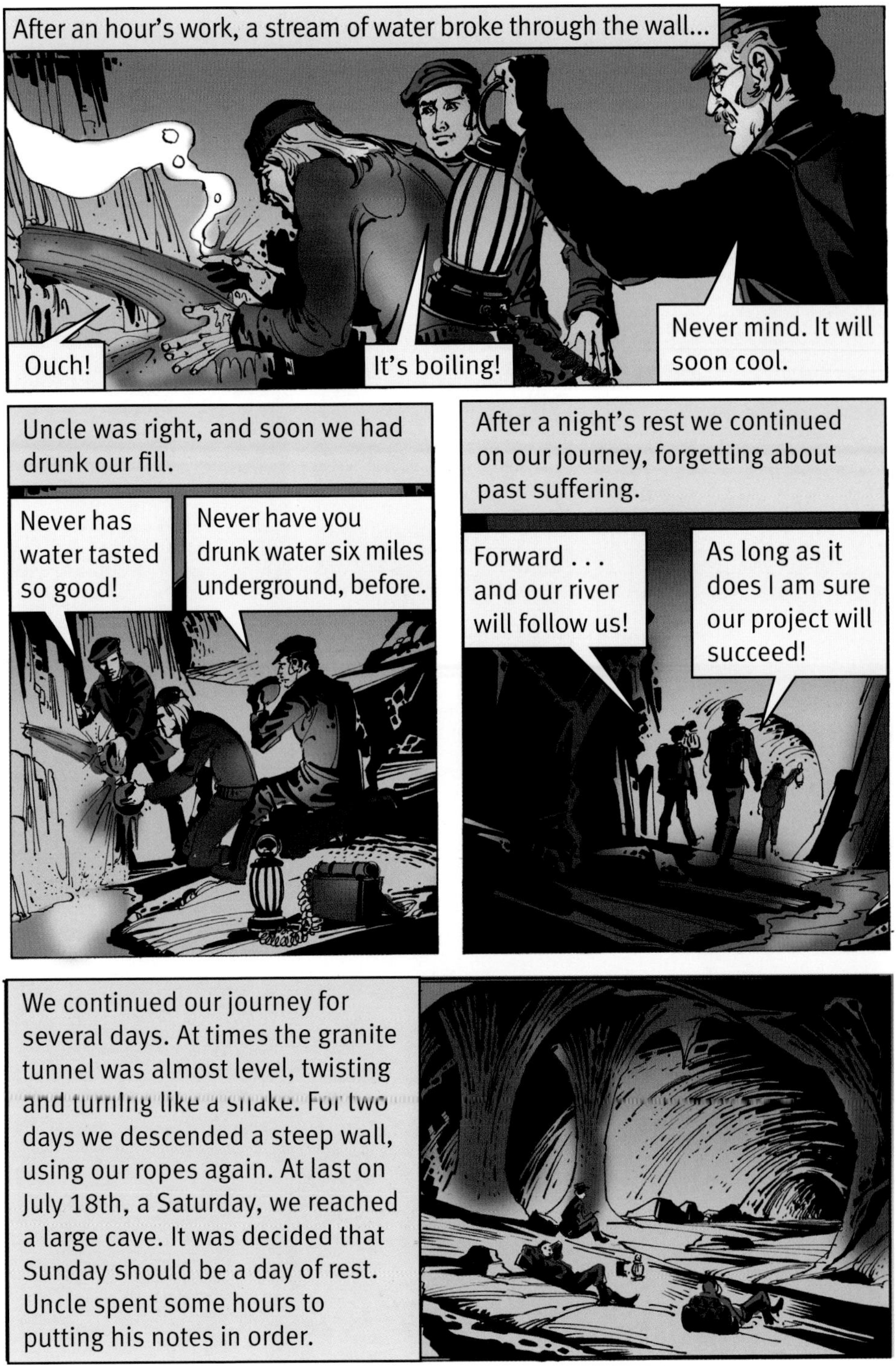
After an hour's work, a stream of water broke through the wall...
Ouch!
It's boiling!
Never mind. It will soon cool.
Uncle was right, and soon we had drunk our fill.
Never has water tasted so good!
Never have you drunk water six miles underground, before.
After a night's rest we continued on our journey, forgetting about past suffering.
Forward . . . and our river will follow us!
As long as it does I am sure our project will succeed!
We continued our journey for several days. At times the granite tunnel was almost level, twisting and turning like a snake. For two days we descended a steep wall, using our ropes again. At last on July 18th, a Saturday, we reached a large cave. It was decided that Sunday should be a day of rest. Uncle spent some hours to putting his notes in order.

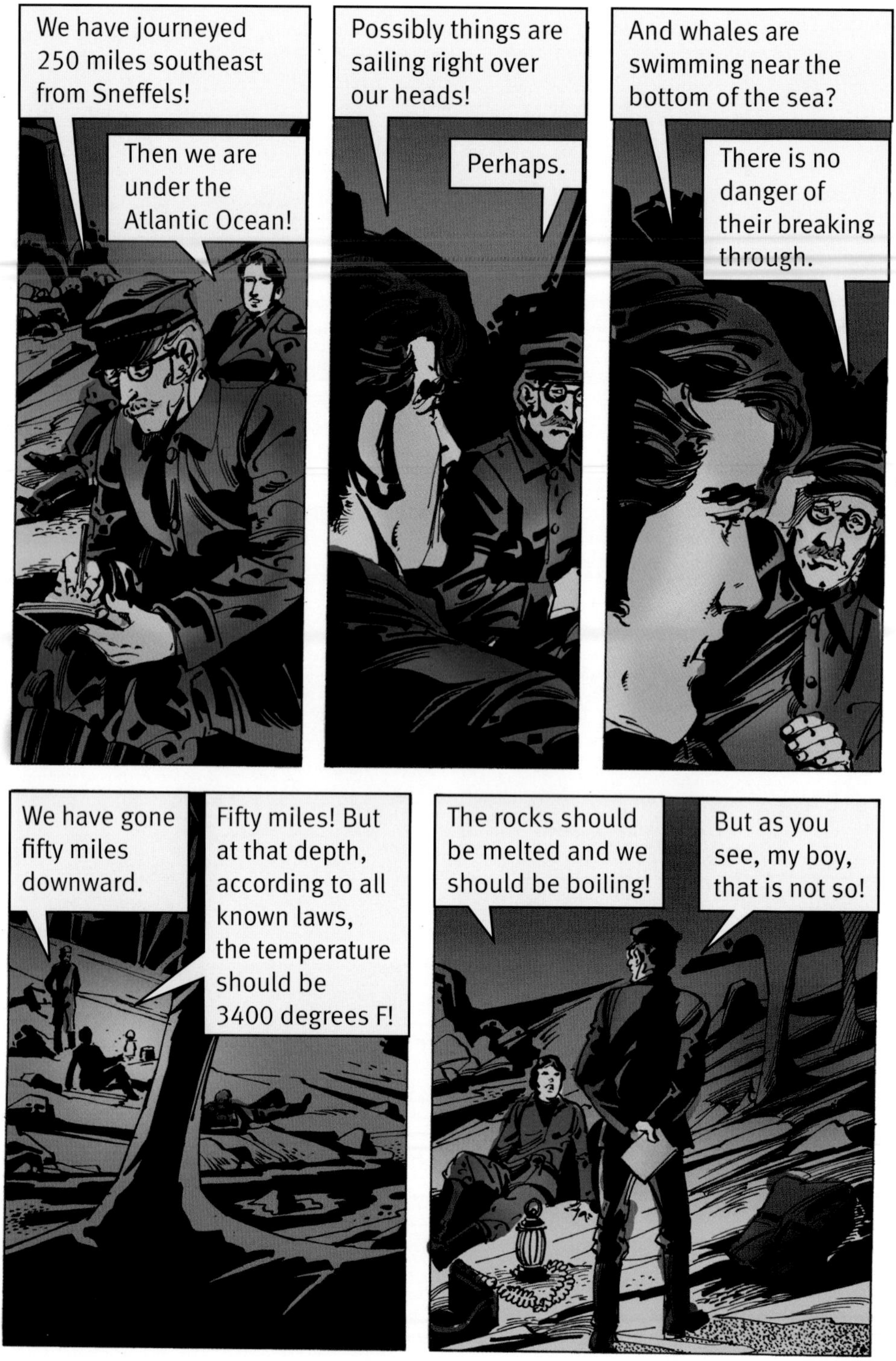
We have journeyed 250 miles southeast from Sneffels!
Then we are under the Atlantic Ocean!
Possibly things are sailing right over our heads!
Perhaps.
And whales are swimming near the bottom of the sea?
There is no danger of their breaking through.
We have gone fifty miles downward.
Fifty miles! But at that depth, according to all known laws, the temperature should be 3400 degrees F!
The rocks should be melted and we should be boiling!
But as you see, my boy, that is not so!

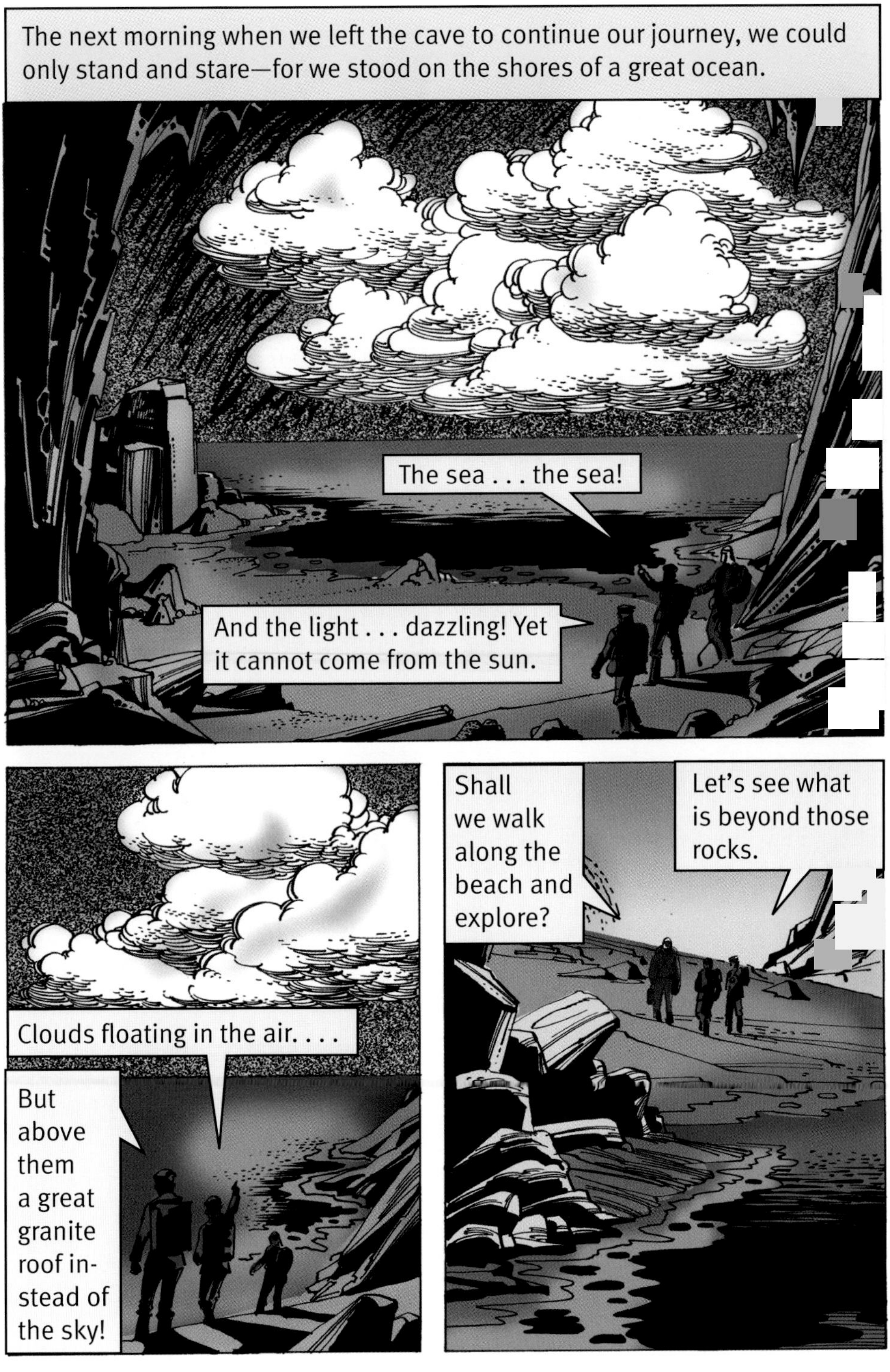
The next morning when we left the cave to continue our journey, we could only stand and stare—for we stood on the shores of a great ocean.
The sea . . . the sea!
And the light . . . dazzling! Yet it cannot come from the sun.
Clouds floating in the air. . . .
But above them a great granite roof in-stead of the sky!
Shall we walk along the beach and explore?
Let's see what is beyond those rocks.

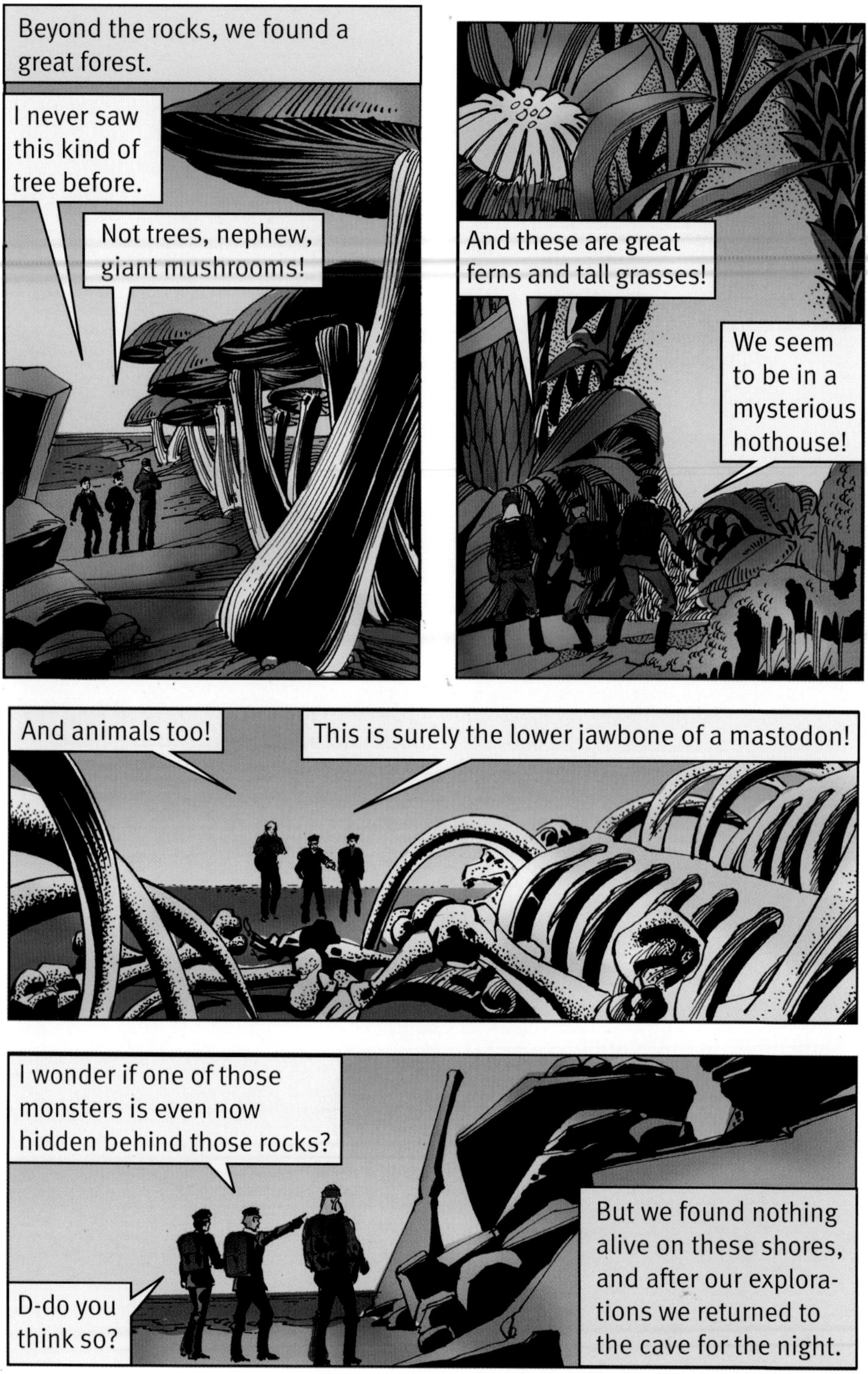
Beyond the rocks, we found a great forest.
I never saw this kind of tree before.
Not trees, nephew, giant mushrooms!
And these are great ferns and tall grasses!
We seem to be in a mysterious hothouse!
And animals too!
This is surely the lower jawbone of a mastodon!
I wonder if one of those monsters is even now hidden behind those rocks?
D-do you think so?
But we found nothing alive on these shores, and after our explora-tions we returned to the cave for the night.

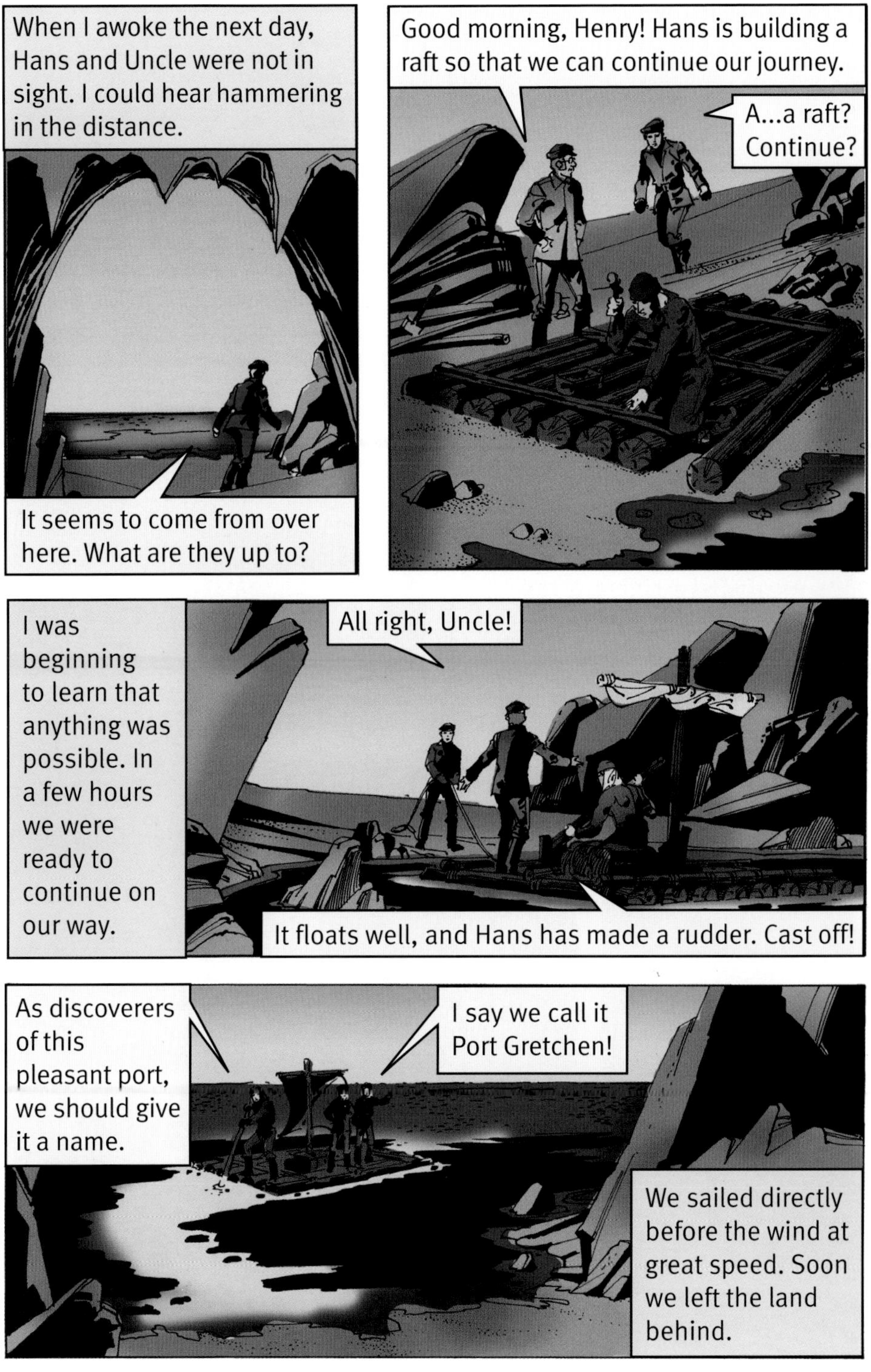
When I awoke the next day, Hans and Uncle were not in sight. I could hear hammering in the distance.
It seems to come from over here. What are they up to?
Good morning, Henry! Hans is building a raft so that we can continue our journey.
A...a raft? Continue?
I was beginning to learn that anything was possible. In a few hours we were ready to continue on our way.
All right, Uncle!
It floats well, and Hans has made a rudder. Cast off!
As discoverers of this pleasant port, we should give it a name.
I say we call it Port Gretchen!
We sailed directly before the wind at great speed. Soon we left the land behind.

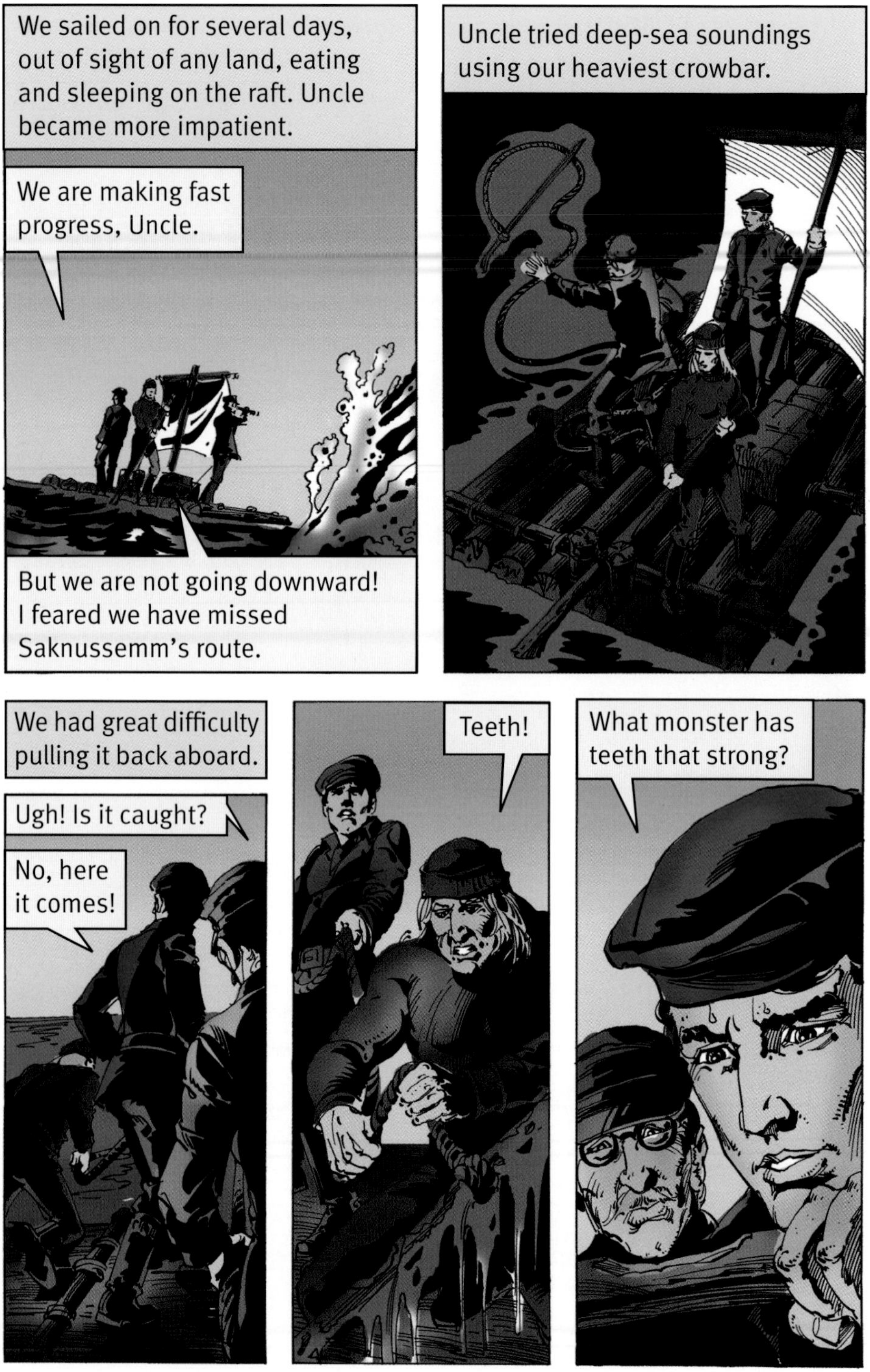
We sailed on for several days, out of sight of any land, eating and sleeping on the raft. Uncle became more impatient.
We are making fast progress, Uncle.
But we are not going downward! I feared we have missed Saknussemm's route.
Uncle tried deep-sea soundings using our heaviest crowbar.
We had great difficulty pulling it back aboard.
Ugh! Is it caught?
No, here it comes!
Teeth!
What monster has teeth that strong?

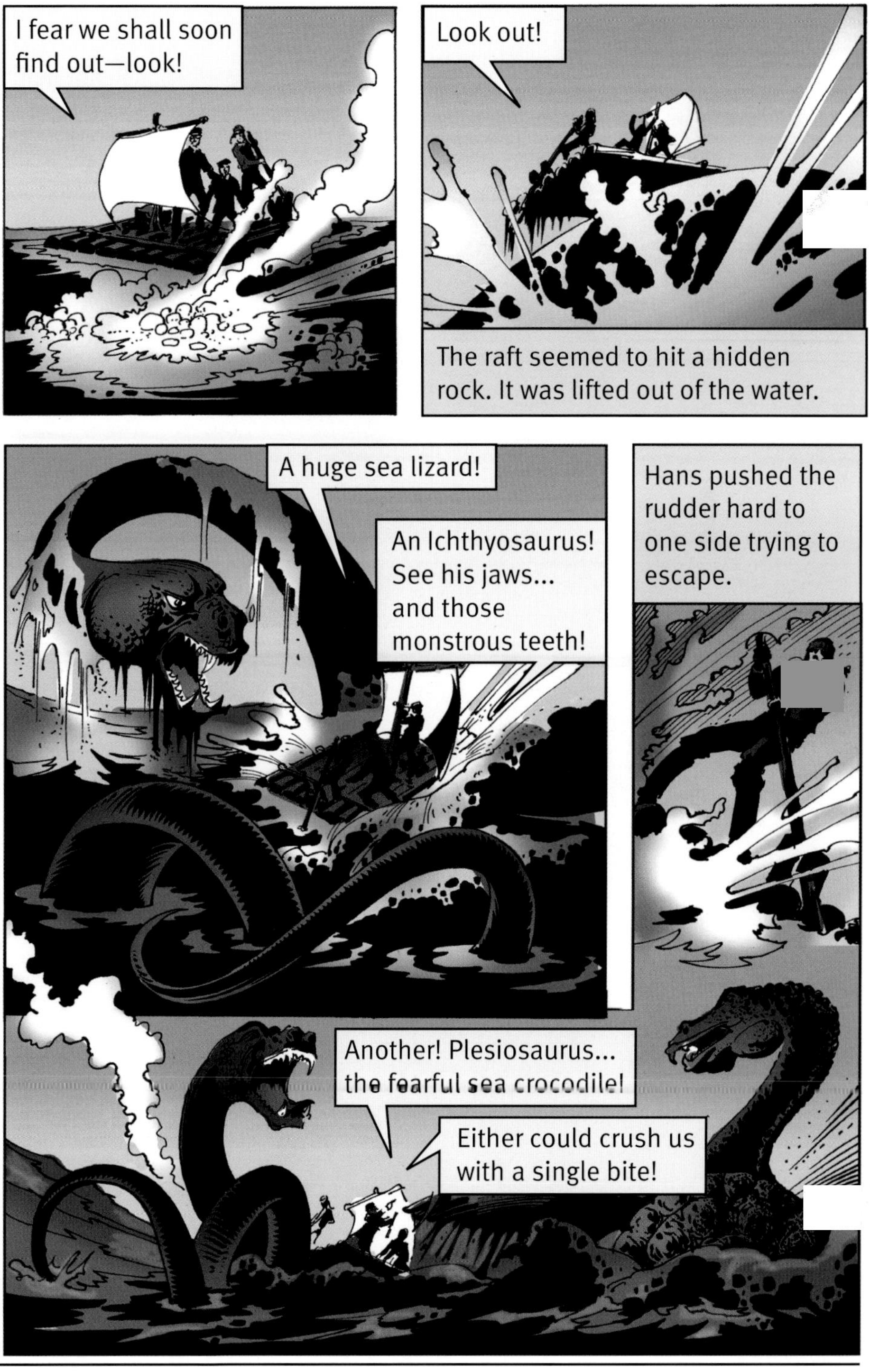
I fear we shall soon find out—look!
Look out!
The raft seemed to hit a hidden rock. It was lifted out of the water.
A huge sea lizard!
An Ichthyosaurus! See his jaws... and those monstrous teeth!
Hans pushed the rudder hard to one side trying to escape.
Another! Plesiosaurus... the fearful sea crocodile!
Either could crush us with a single bite!

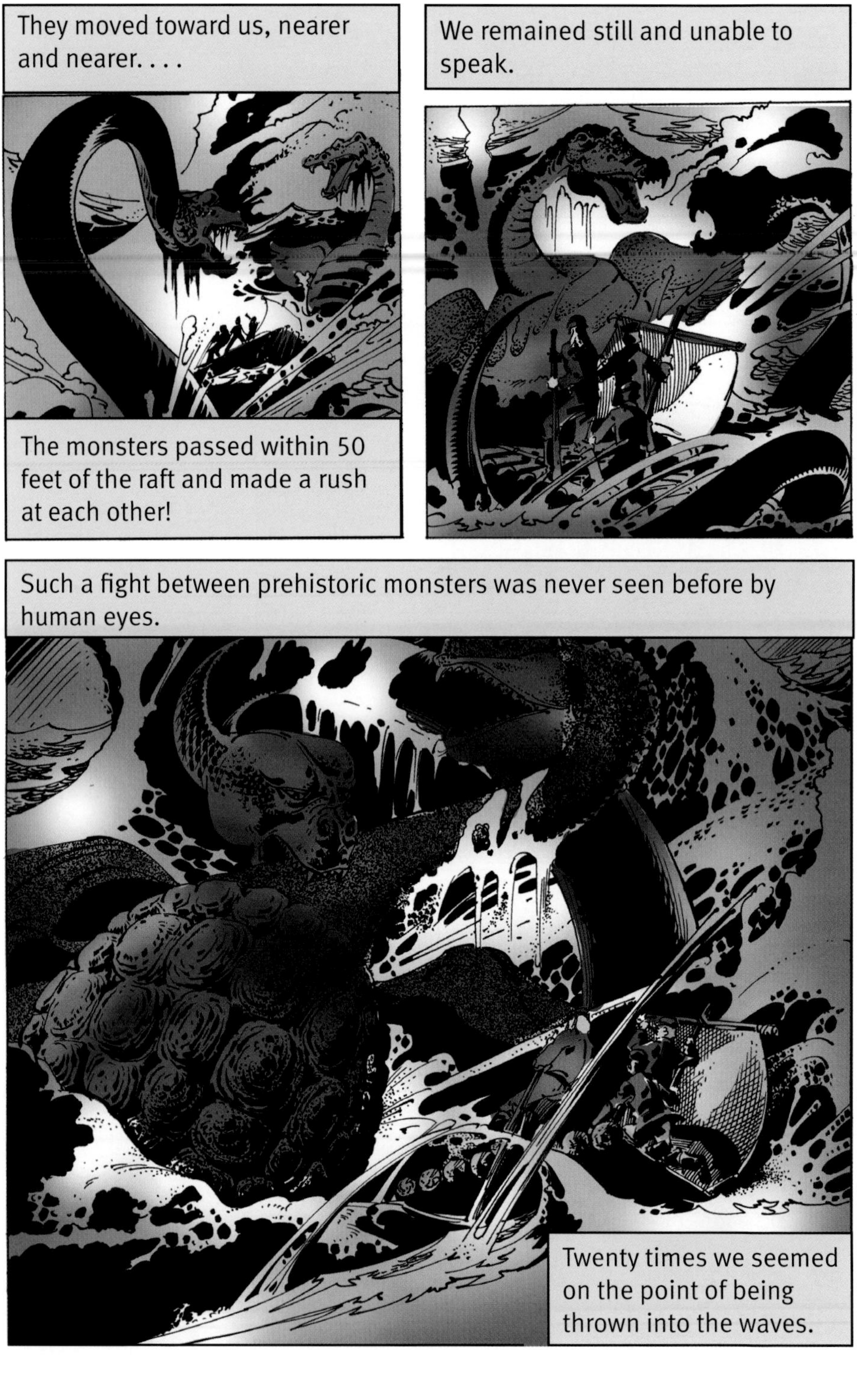
They moved toward us, nearer and nearer. . . .
The monsters passed within 50 feet of the raft and made a rush at each other!
We remained still and unable to speak.
Such a fight between prehistoric monsters was never seen before by human eyes.
Twenty times we seemed on the point of being thrown into the waves.

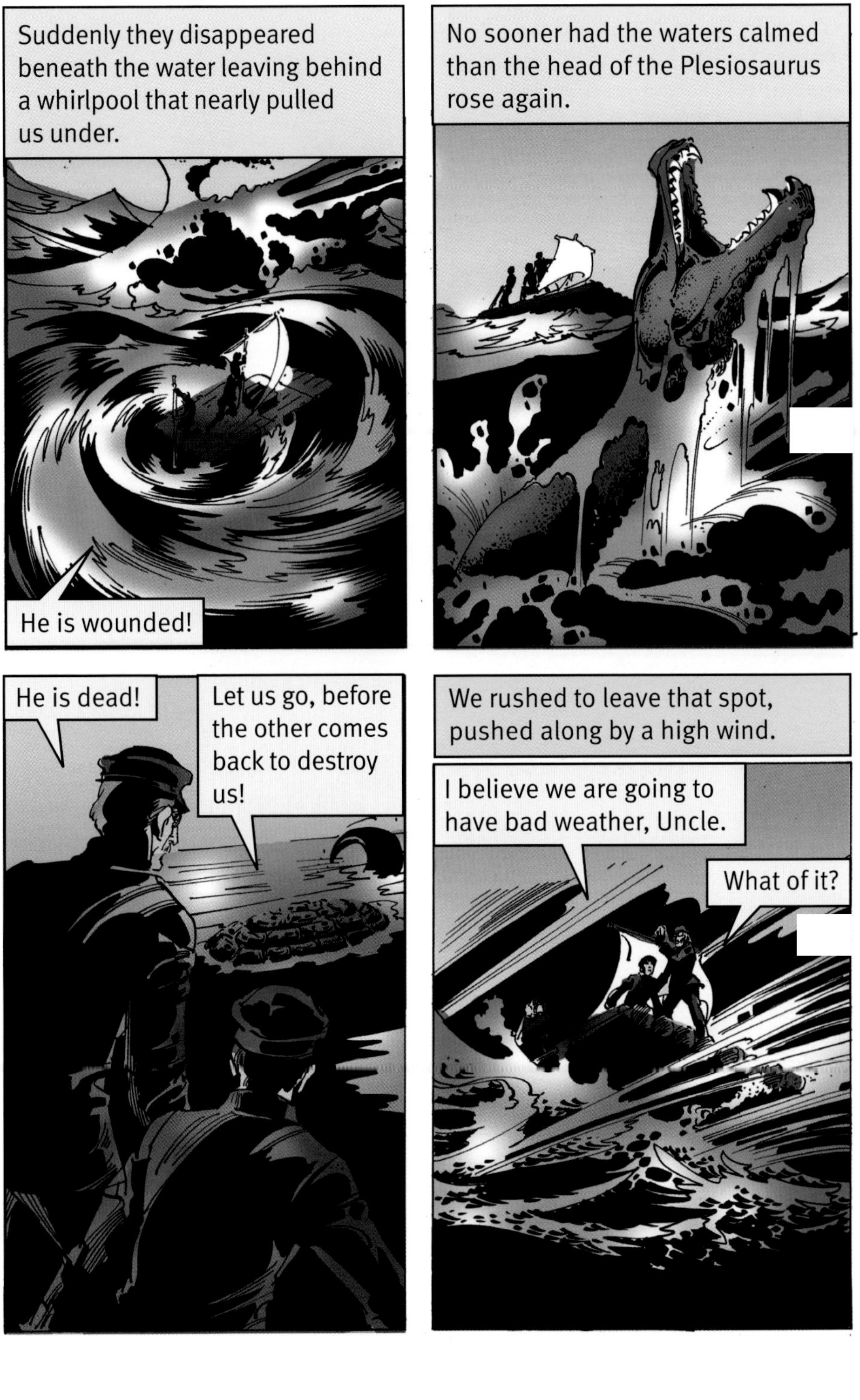
Suddenly they disappeared beneath the water leaving behind a whirlpool that nearly pulled us under.
He is wounded!
No sooner had the waters calmed than the head of the Plesiosaurus rose again.
He is dead!
Let us go, before the other comes back to destroy us!
We rushed to leave that spot, pushed along by a high wind.
I believe we are going to have bad weather, Uncle.
What of it?

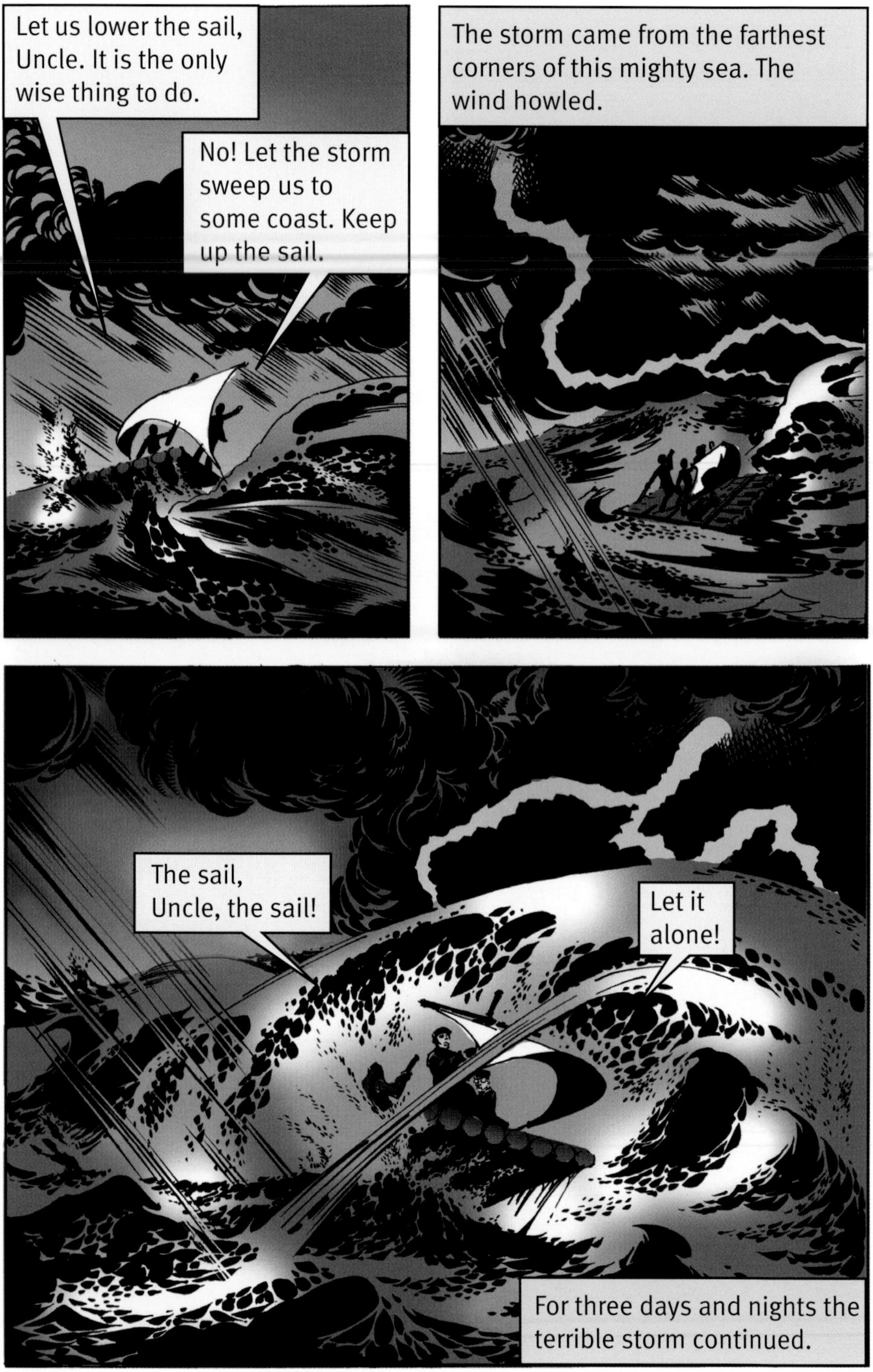
Let us lower the sail, Uncle. It is the only wise thing to do.
No! Let the storm sweep us to some coast. Keep up the sail.
The storm came from the farthest corners of this mighty sea. The wind howled.
The sail, Uncle, the sail!
Let it alone!
For three days and nights the terrible storm continued.

Lightning flashed all around and hit our mast.

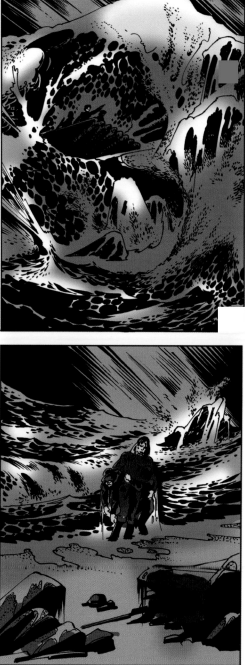

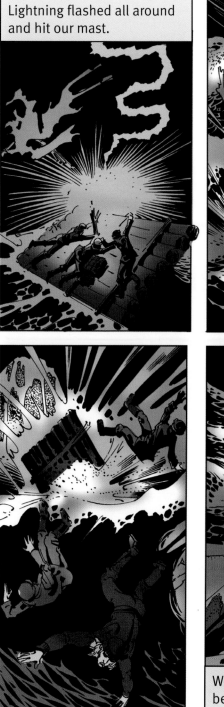

We wouldn't have lived if it hadn't been for Hans.

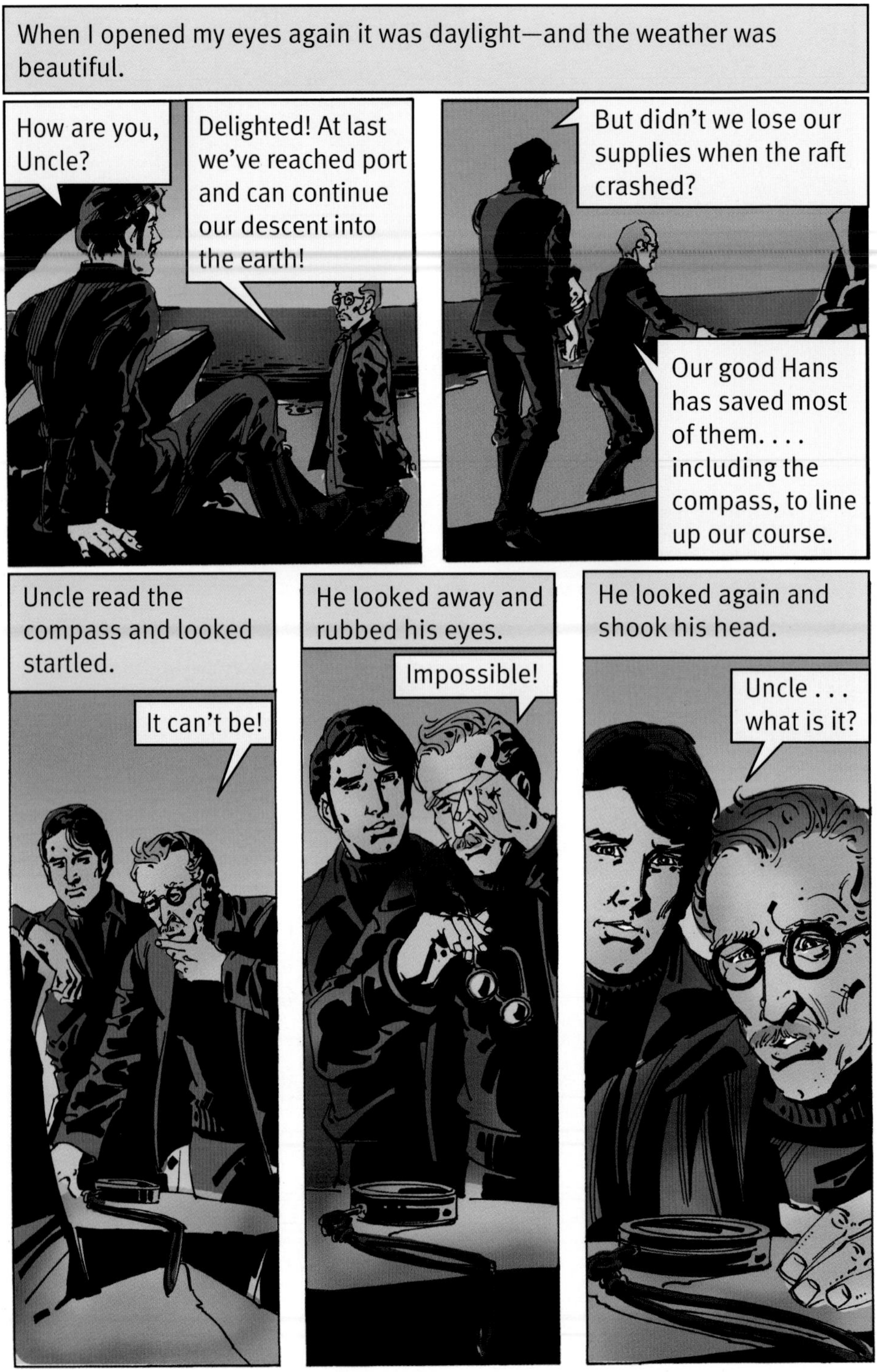
When I opened my eyes again it was daylight—and the weather was beautiful.
How are you, Uncle?
Delighted! At last we've reached port and can continue our descent into the earth!
But didn't we lose our supplies when the raft crashed?
Our good Hans has saved most of them. . . . including the compass, to line up our course.
Uncle read the compass and looked startled.
It can't be!
He looked away and rubbed his eyes.
Impossible!
He looked again and shook his head.
Uncle . . . what is it?

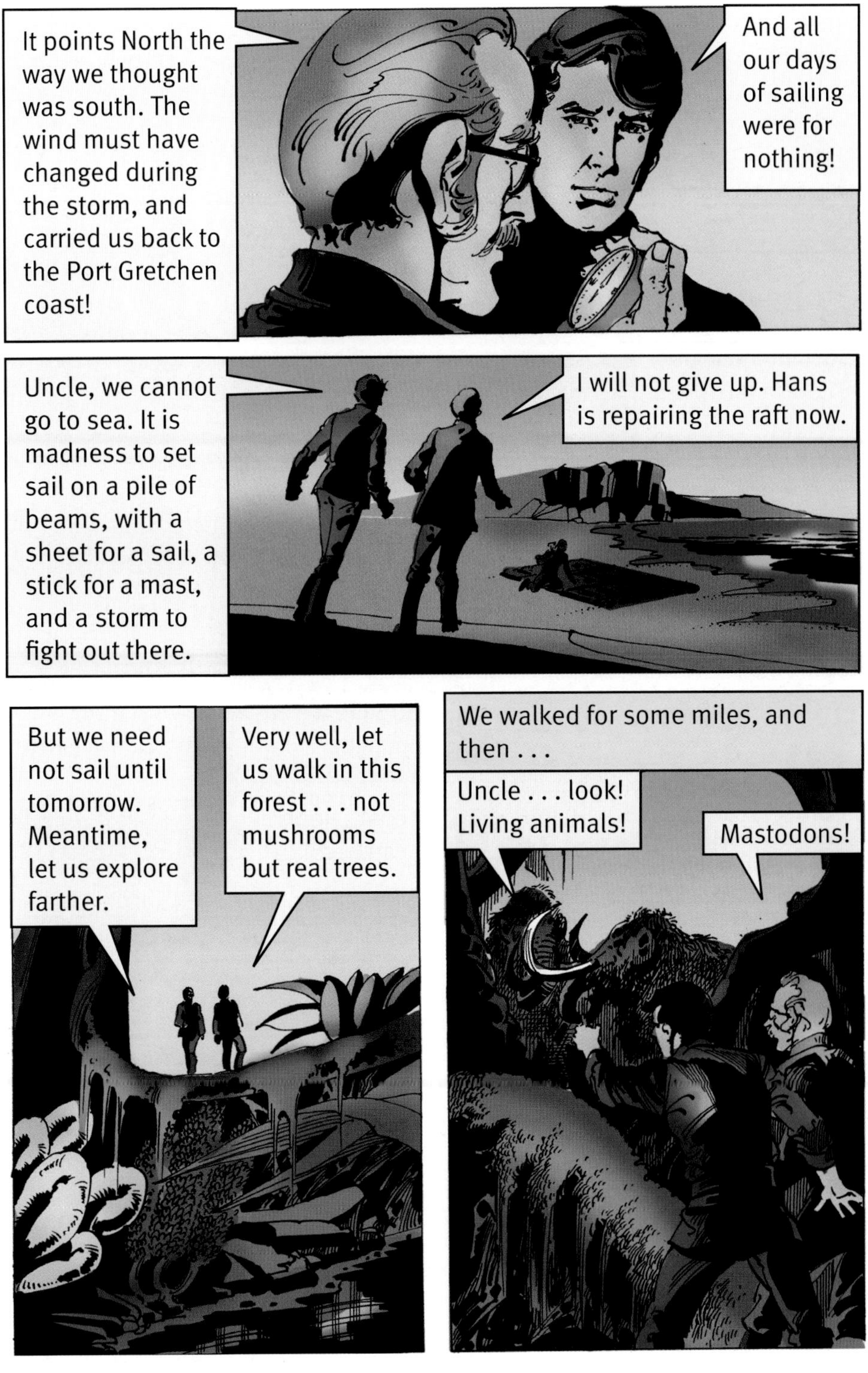
It points North the way we thought was south. The wind must have changed during the storm, and carried us back to the Port Gretchen coast!
And all our days of sailing were for nothing!
Uncle, we cannot go to sea. It is madness to set sail on a pile of beams, with a sheet for a sail, a stick for a mast, and a storm to fight out there.
I will not give up. Hans is repairing the raft now.
But we need not sail until tomorrow. Meantime, let us explore farther.
Very well, let us walk in this forest . . . not mushrooms but real trees.
We walked for some miles, and then . . .
Uncle . . . look! Living animals!
Mastodons!

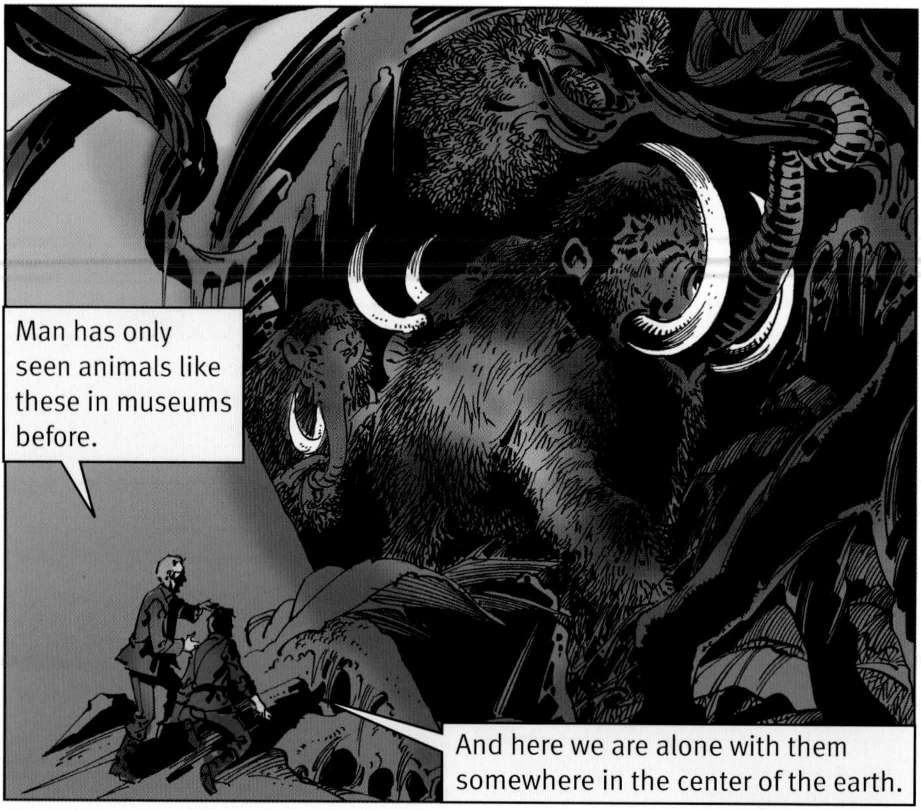
Man has only seen animals like these in museums before.
And here we are alone with them somewhere in the center of the earth.

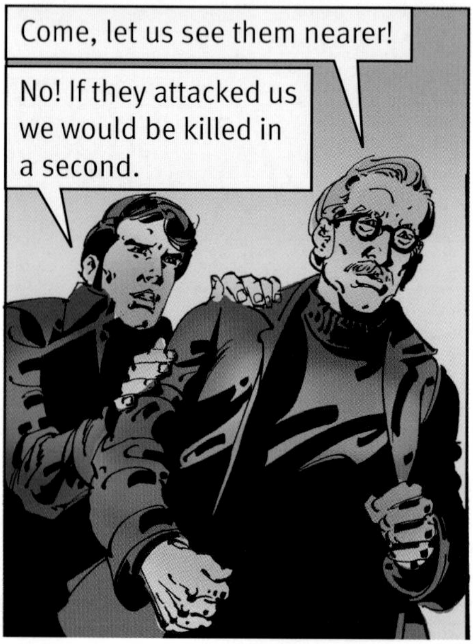
Come, let us see them nearer!
No! If they attacked us we would be killed in a second.

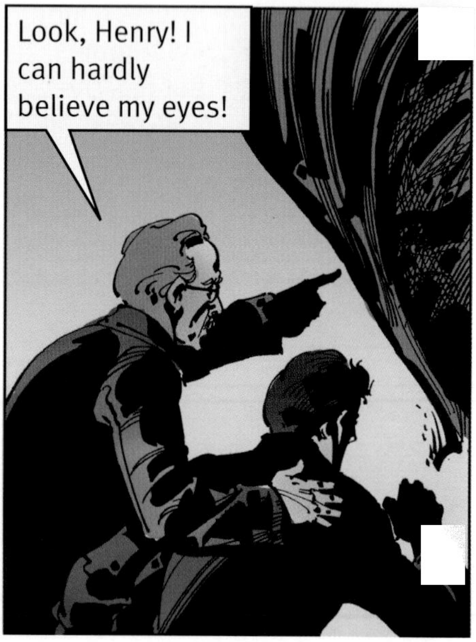
Look, Henry! I can hardly believe my eyes!

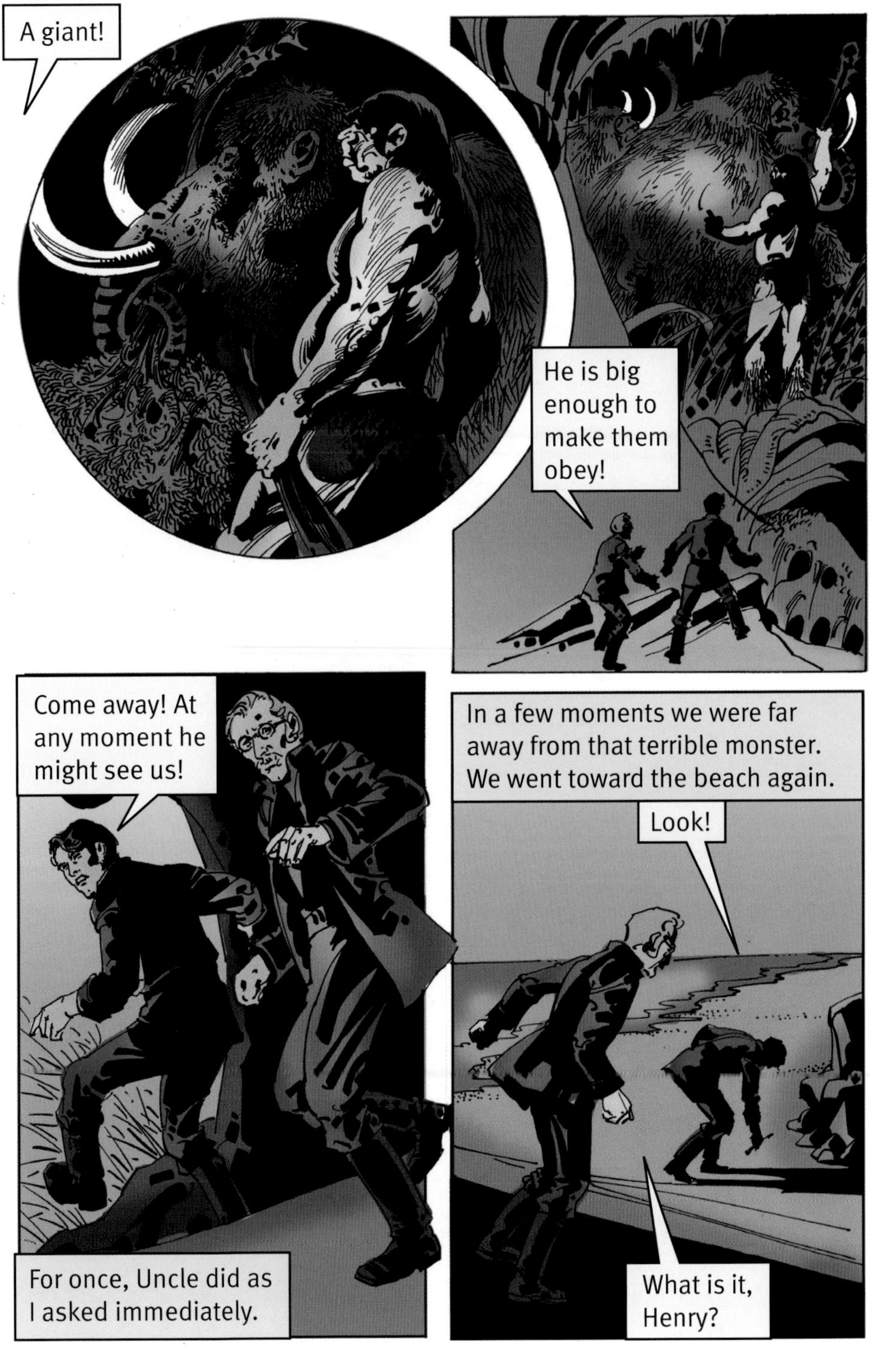
A giant!
He is big enough to make them obey!
Come away! At any moment he might see us!
For once, Uncle did as I asked immediately.
In a few moments we were far away from that terrible monster. We went toward the beach again.
Look!
What is it, Henry?

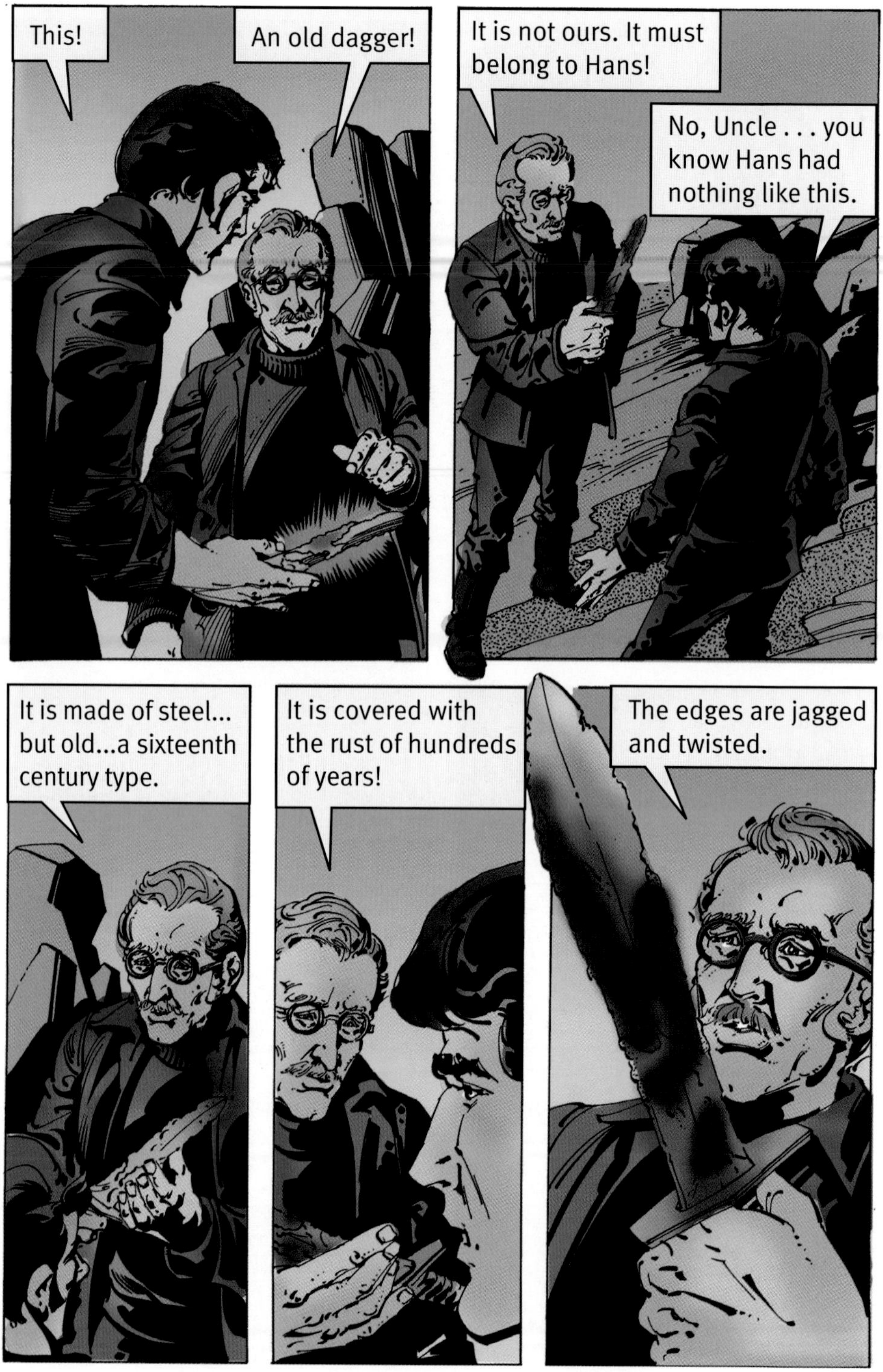
This!
An old dagger!
It is not ours. It must belong to Hans!
No, Uncle . . . you know Hans had nothing like this.
It is made of steel... but old...a sixteenth century type.
It is covered with the rust of hundreds of years!
The edges are jagged and twisted.

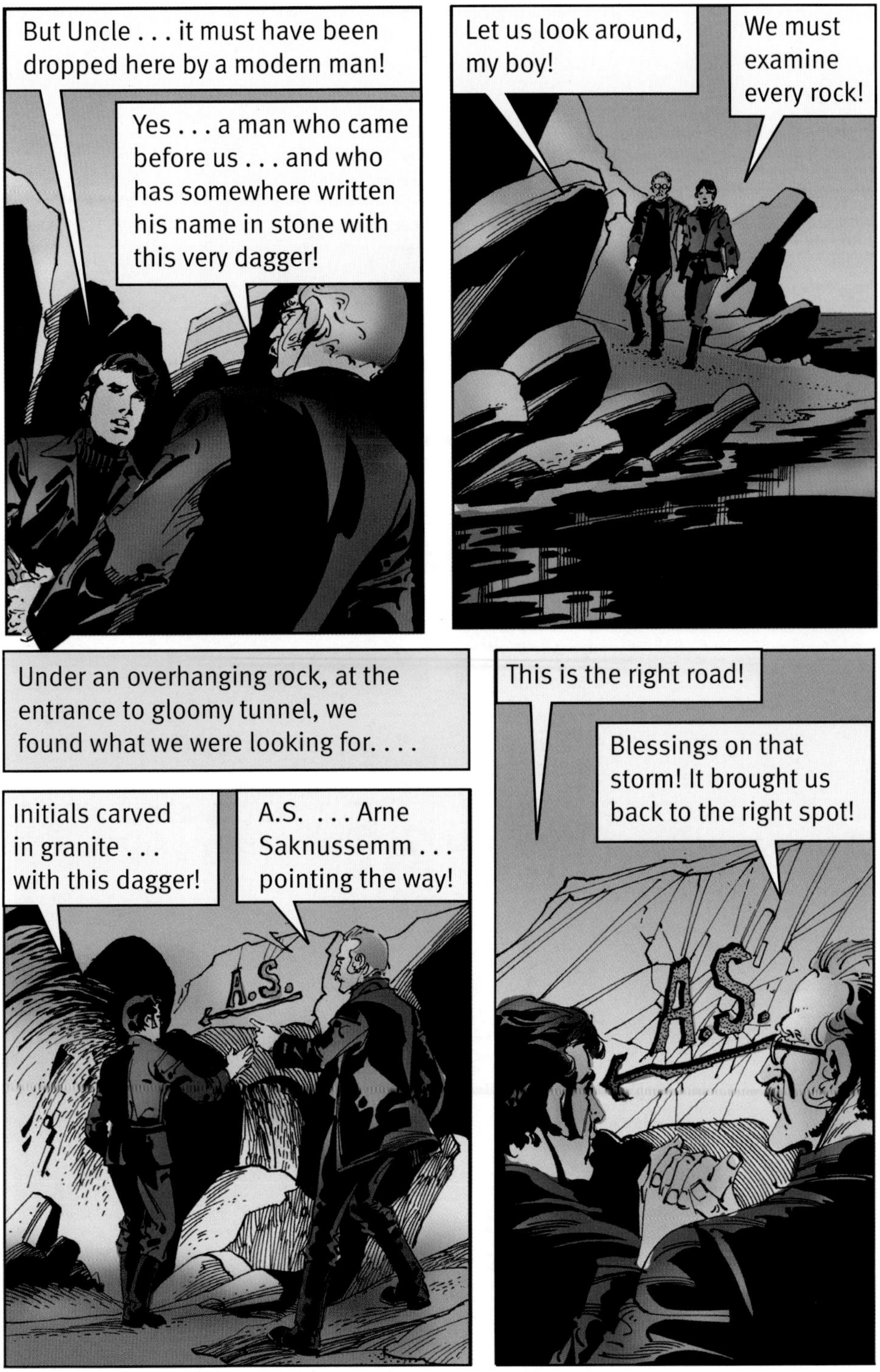
But Uncle . . . it must have been dropped here by a modern man!
Yes . . . a man who came before us . . . and who has somewhere written his name in stone with this very dagger!
Let us look around, my boy!
We must examine every rock!
Under an overhanging rock, at the entrance to gloomy tunnel, we found what we were looking for. . . .
Initials carved in granite . . . with this dagger!
A.S. . . . Arne Saknussemm . . . pointing the way!
A.S.
This is the right road!
Blessings on that storm! It brought us back to the right spot!
A.S.

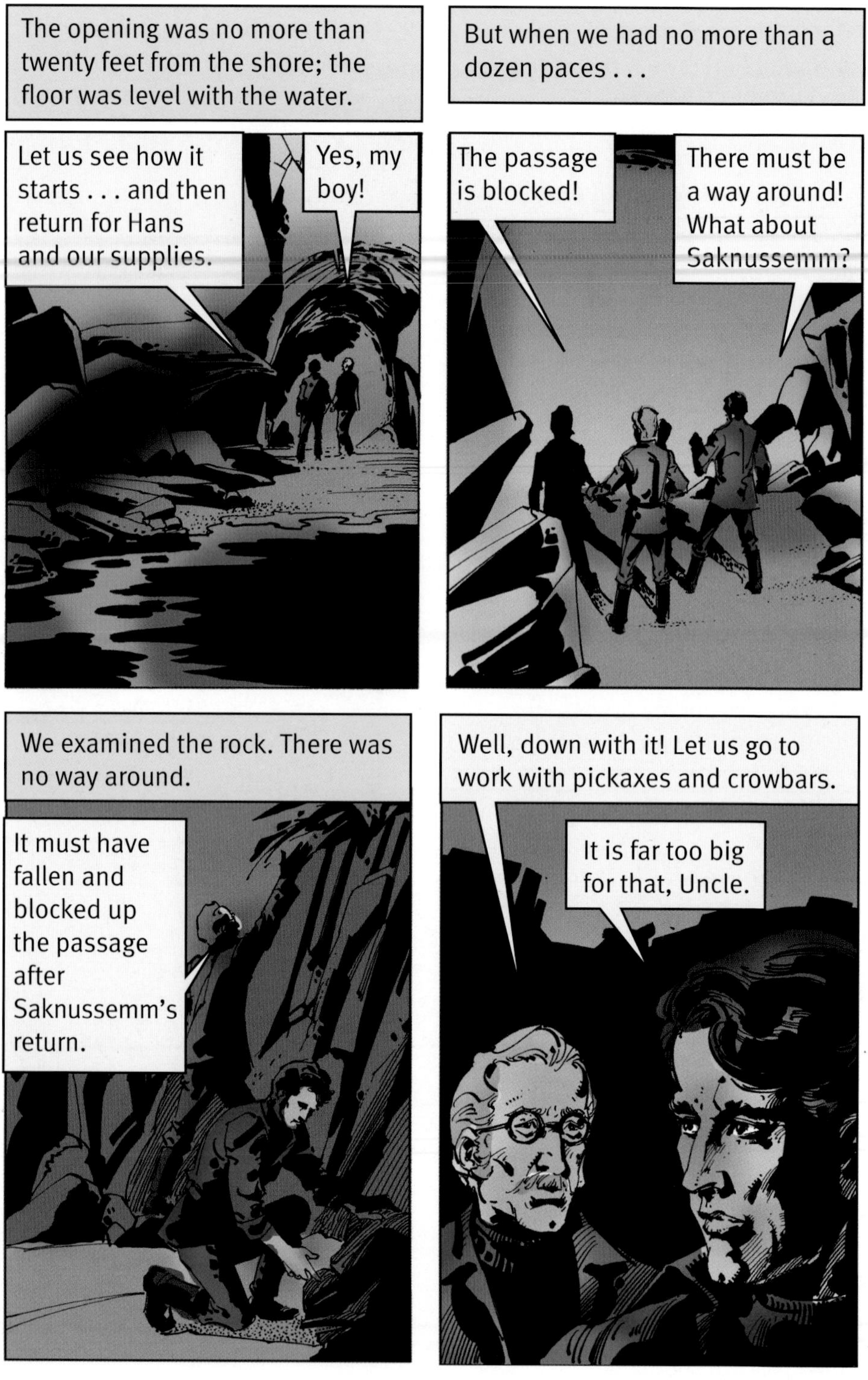
The opening was no more than twenty feet from the shore; the floor was level with the water.
Let us see how it starts . . . and then return for Hans and our supplies.
Yes, my boy!
But when we had no more than a dozen paces . . .
The passage is blocked!
There must be a way around! What about Saknussemm?
We examined the rock. There was no way around.
It must have fallen and blocked up the passage after Saknussemm's return.
Well, down with it! Let us go to work with pickaxes and crowbars.
It is far too big for that, Uncle.

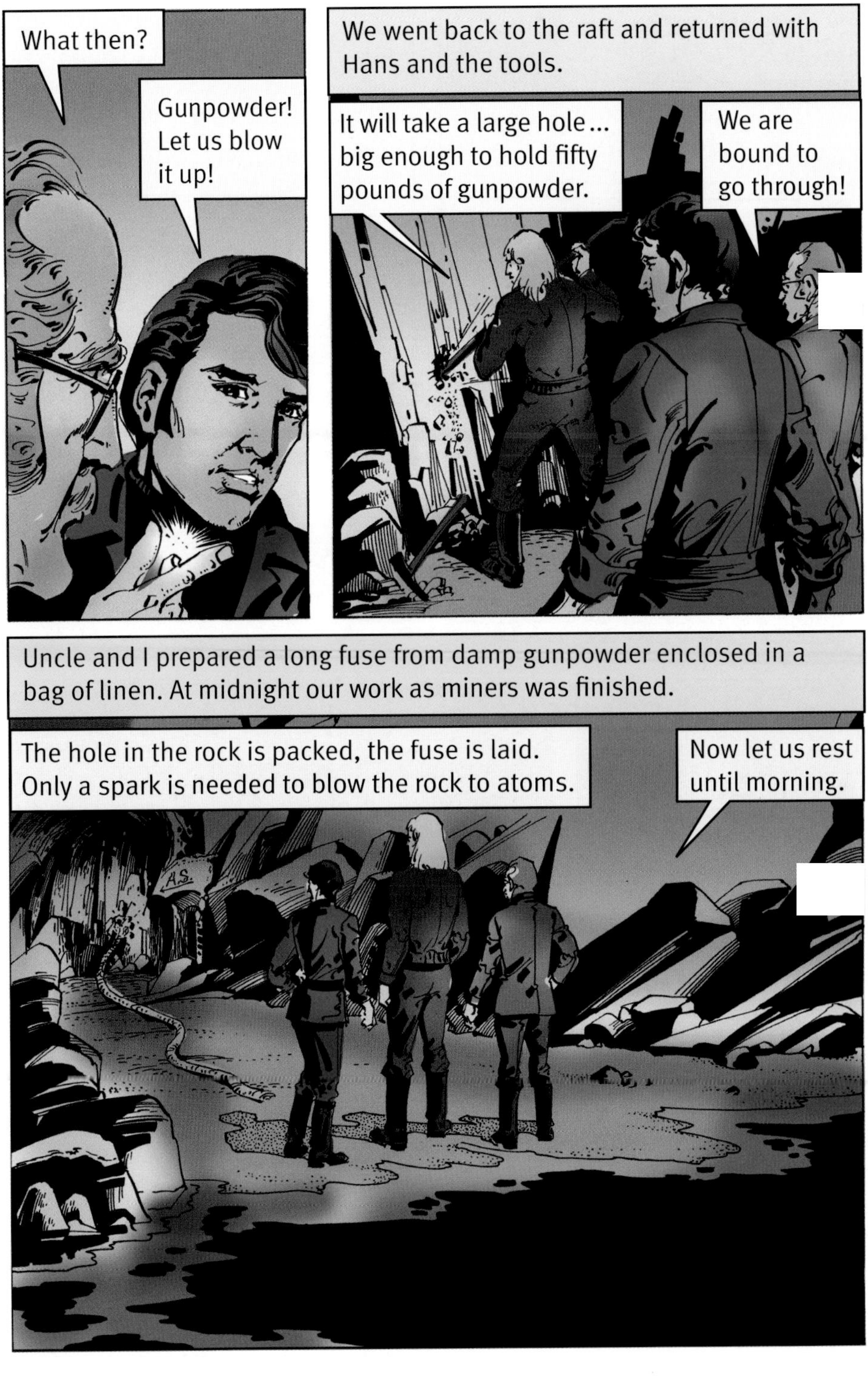
What then?
Gunpowder! Let us blow it up!
We went back to the raft and returned with Hans and the tools.
It will take a large hole... big enough to hold fifty pounds of gunpowder.
We are bound to go through!
Uncle and I prepared a long fuse from damp gunpowder enclosed in a bag of linen. At midnight our work as miners was finished.
The hole in the rock is packed, the fuse is laid. Only a spark is needed to blow the rock to atoms.
Now let us rest until morning.
A.S.

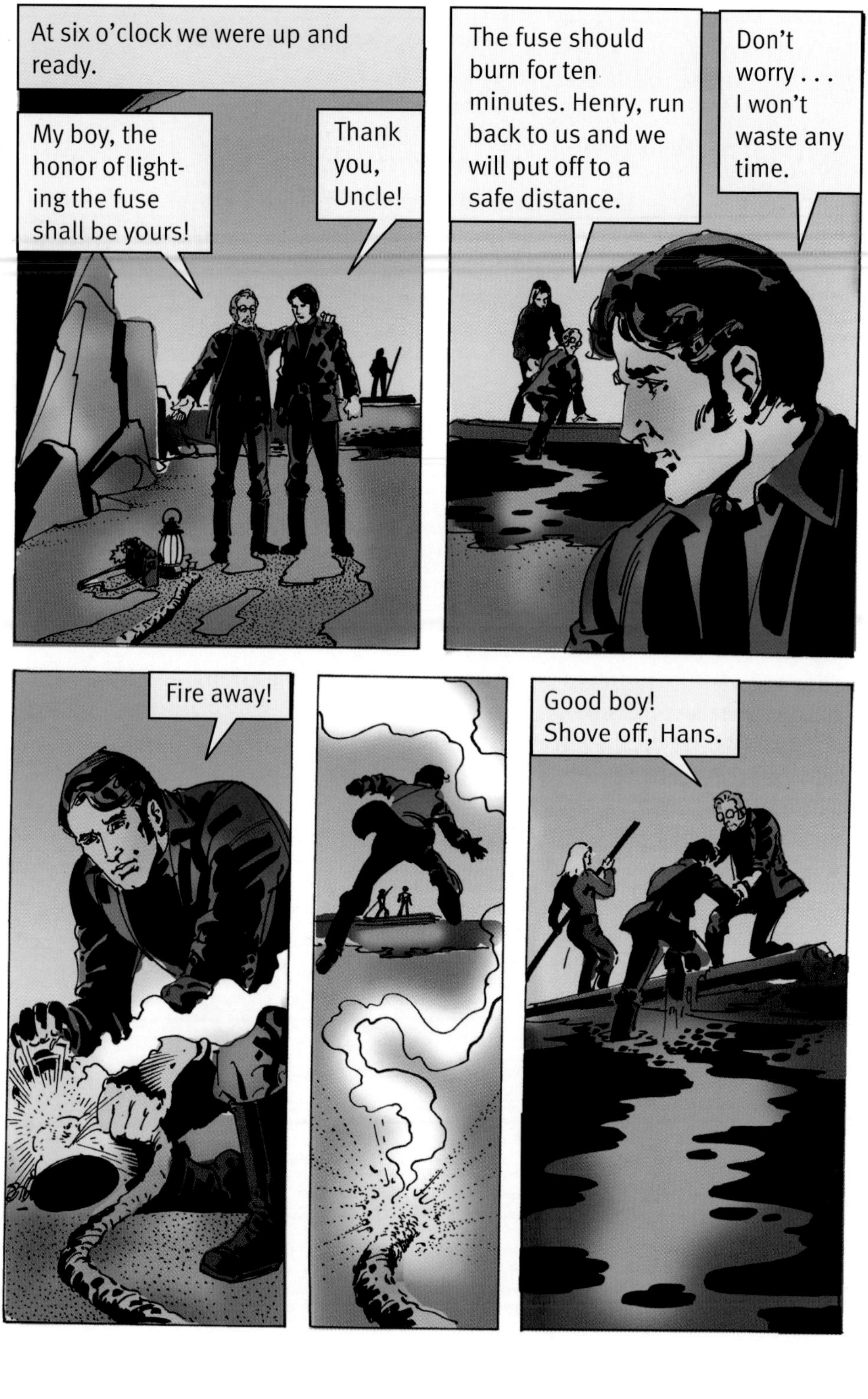
At six o'clock we were up and ready.
My boy, the honor of light-ing the fuse shall be yours!
Thank you, Uncle!
The fuse should burn for ten minutes. Henry, run back to us and we will put off to a safe distance.
Don't worry . . . I won't waste any time.
Fire away!
Good boy! Shove off, Hans.

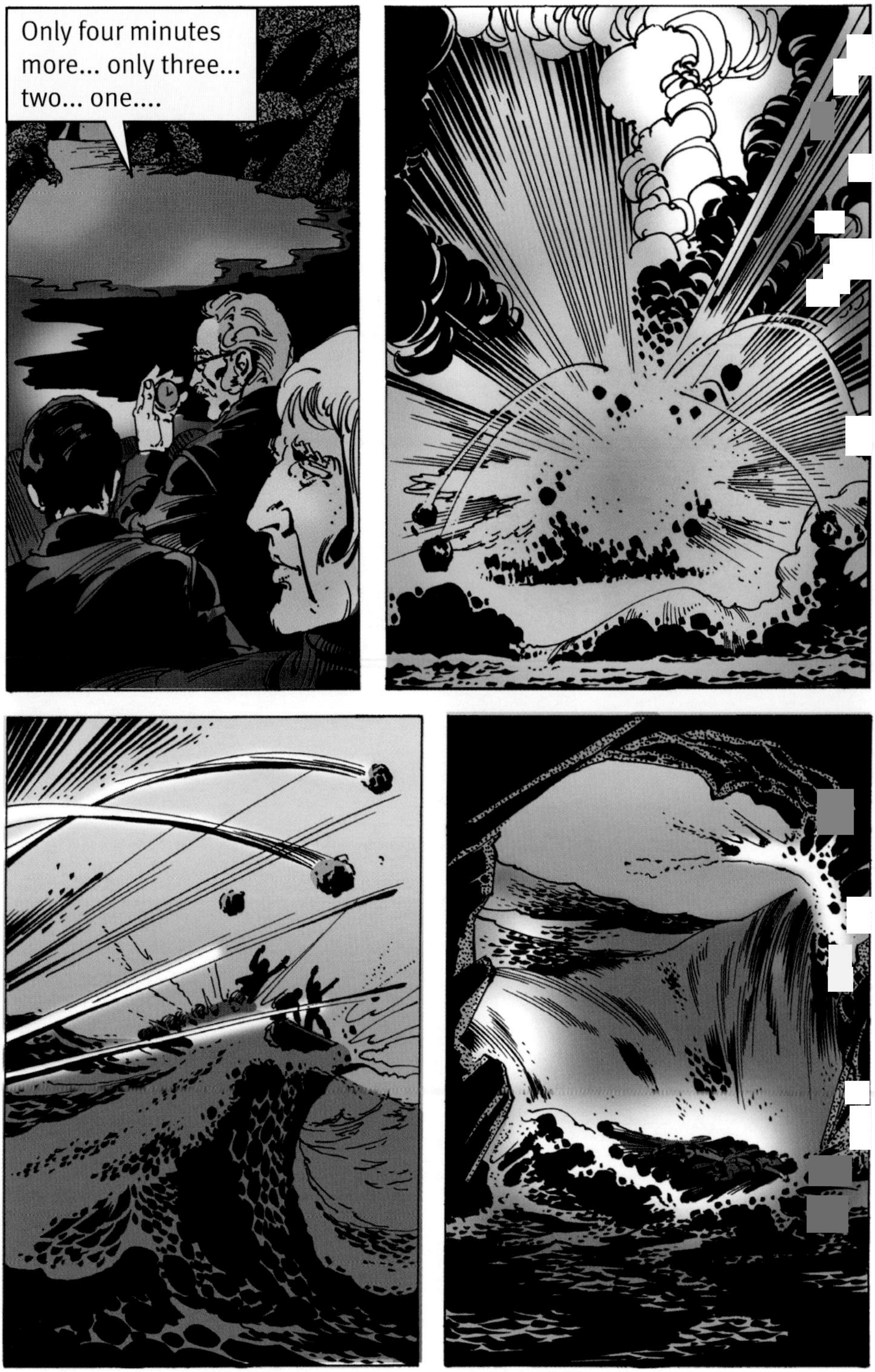
Only four minutes more... only three... two... one....

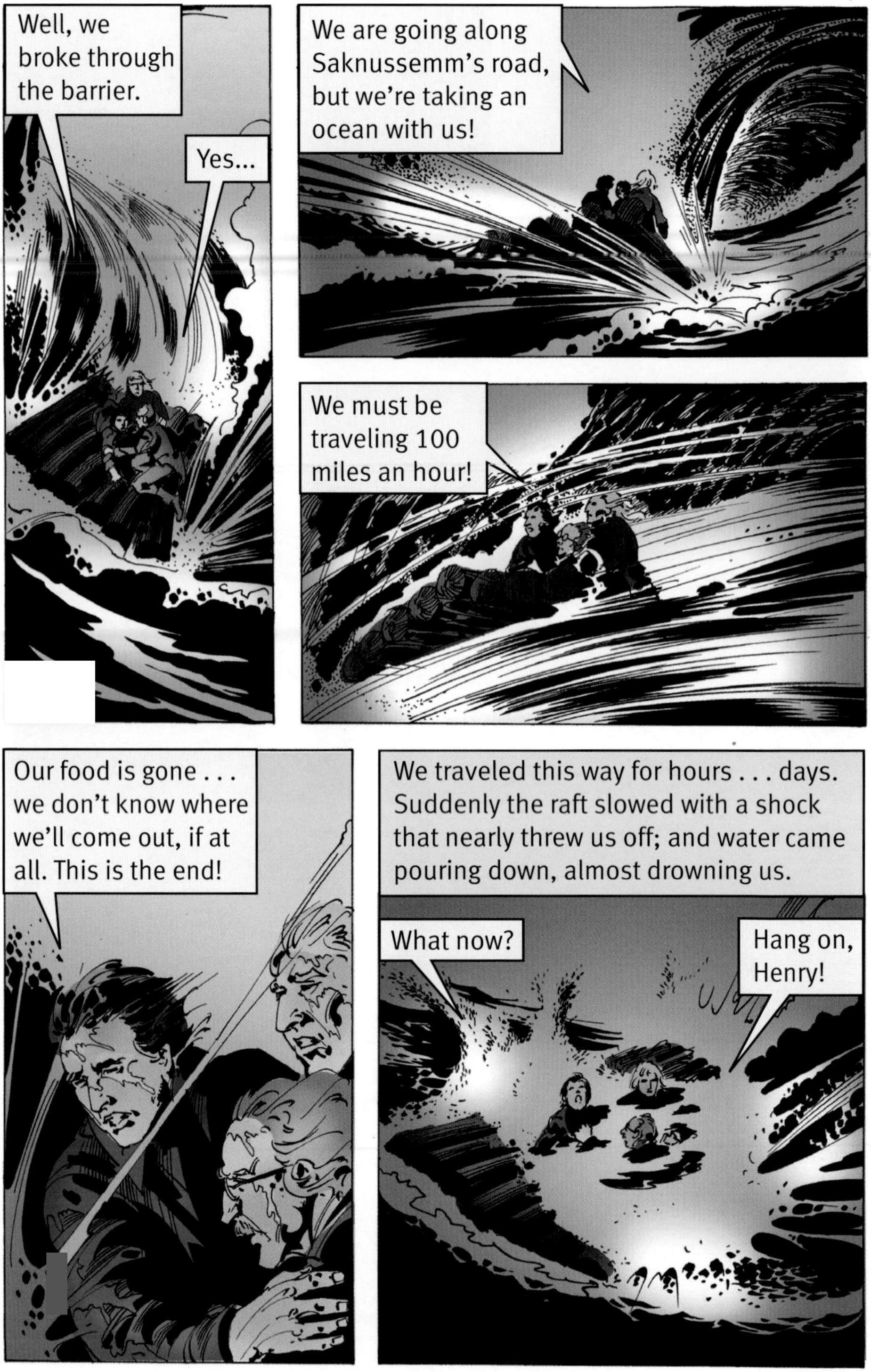
Well, we broke through the barrier.
Yes...
We are going along Saknussemm's road, but we're taking an ocean with us!
We must be traveling 100 miles an hour!
Our food is gone . . . we don't know where we'll come out, if at all. This is the end!
We traveled this way for hours . . . days. Suddenly the raft slowed with a shock that nearly threw us off; and water came pouring down, almost drowning us.
What now?
Hang on, Henry!

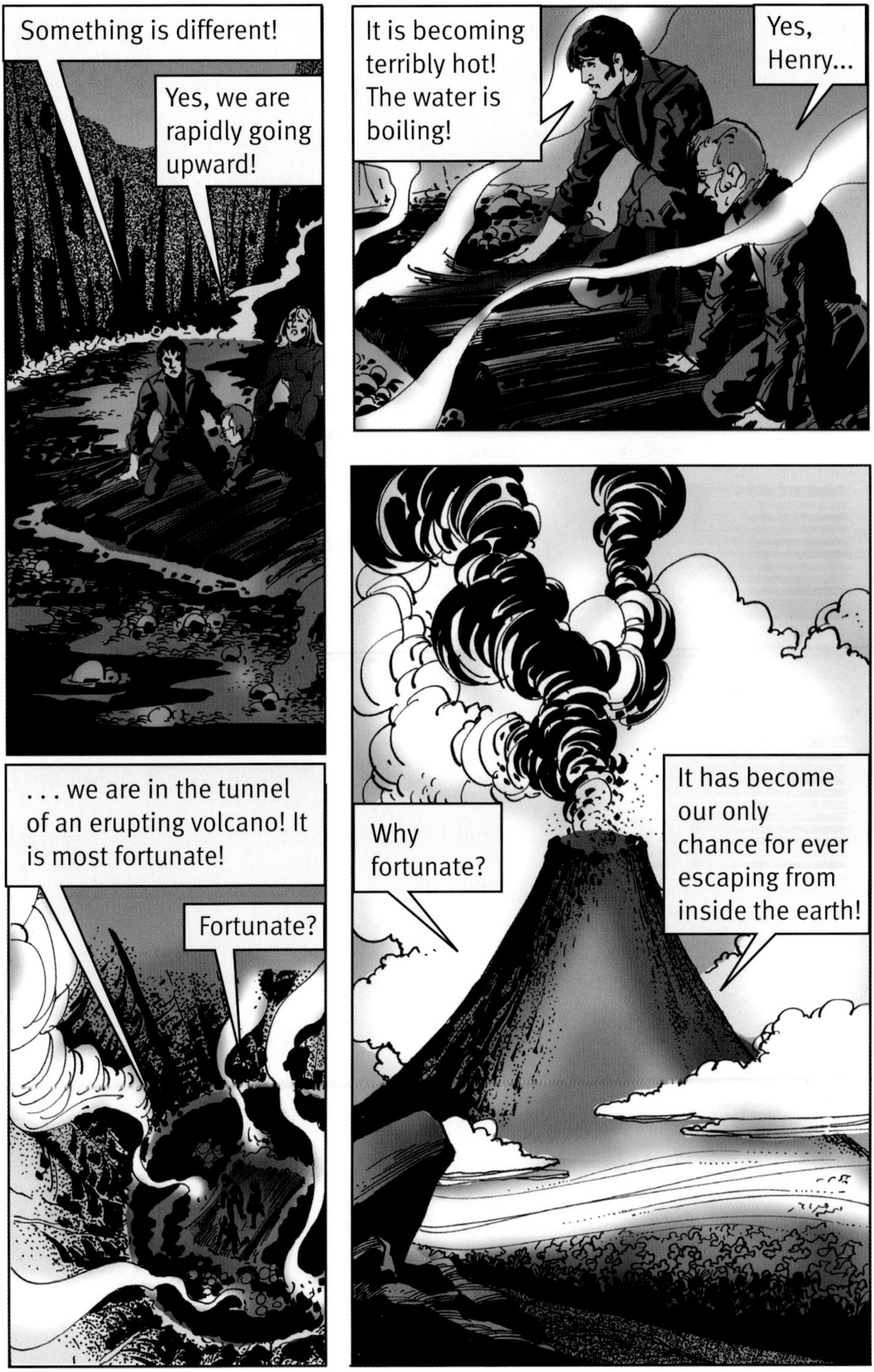
Something is different!
Yes, we are rapidly going upward!
It is becoming terribly hot! The water is boiling!
Yes, Henry...
. . . we are in the tunnel of an erupting volcano! It is most fortunate!
Fortunate?
Why fortunate?
It has become our only chance for ever escaping from inside the earth!

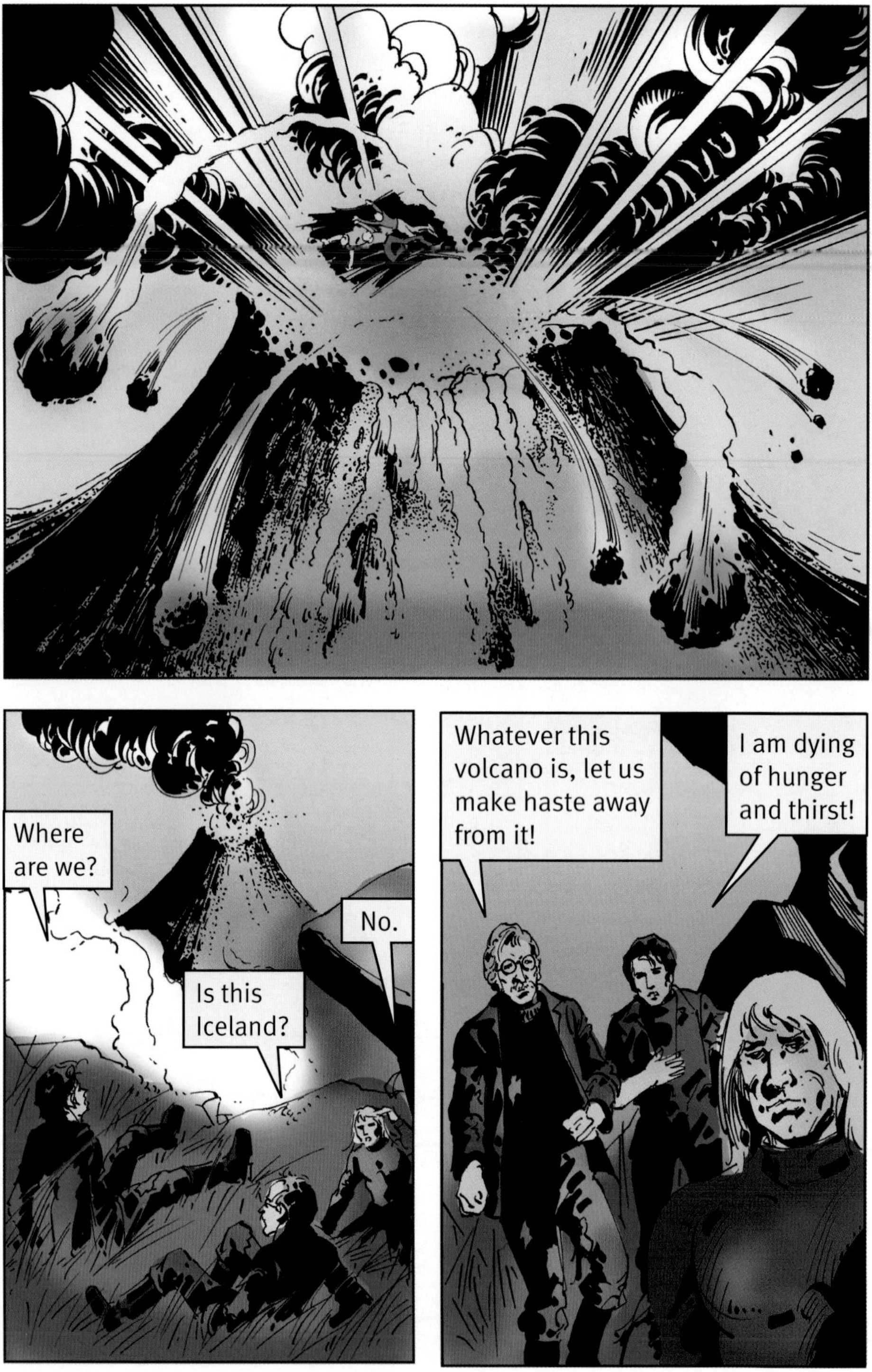
Where are we?
Is this Iceland?
No.
Whatever this volcano is, let us make haste away from it!
I am dying of hunger and thirst!

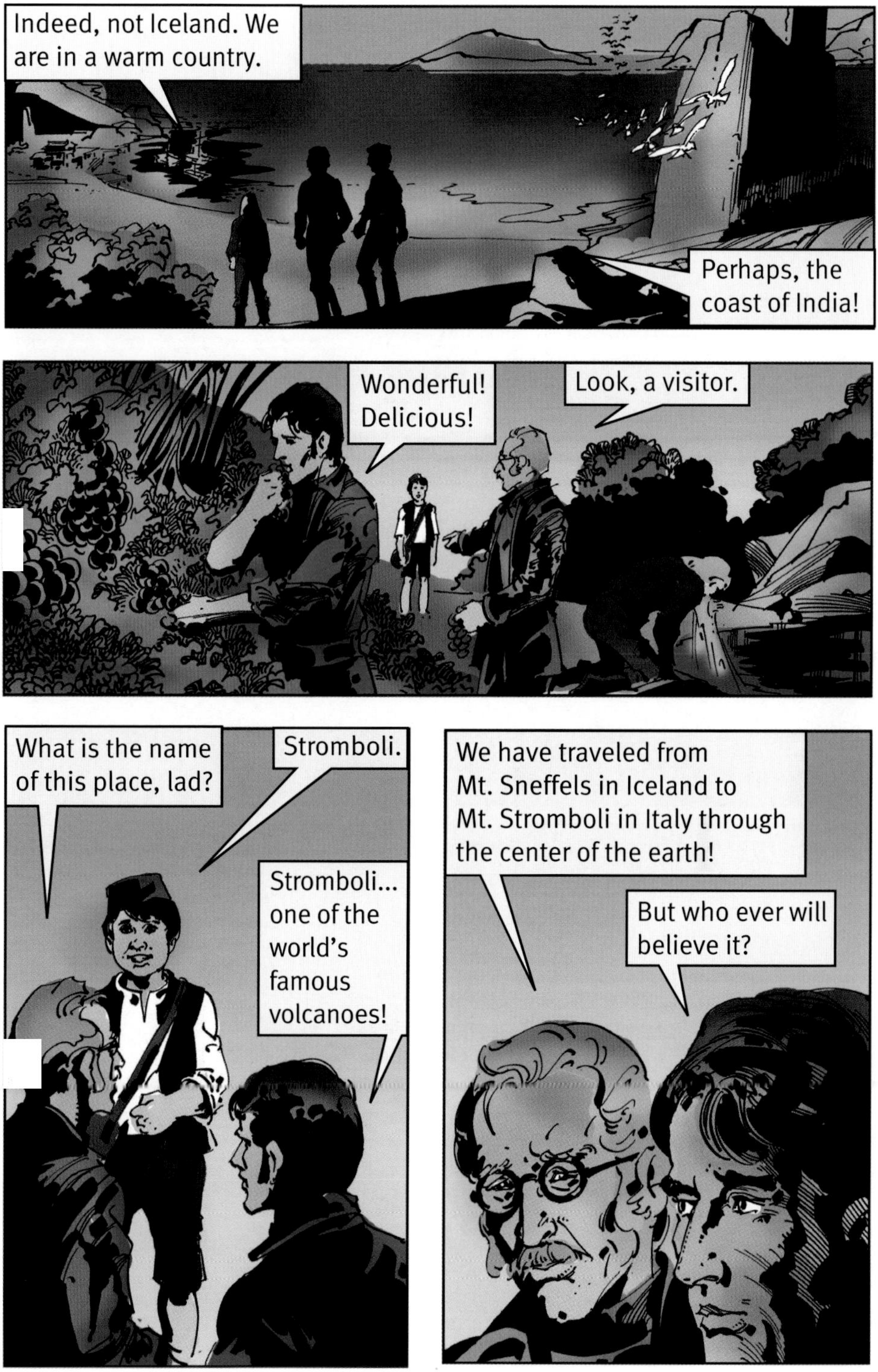
Indeed, not Iceland. We are in a warm country.
Perhaps, the coast of India!
Wonderful! Delicious!
Look, a visitor.
What is the name of this place, lad?
Stromboli.
Stromboli... one of the world's famous volcanoes!
We have traveled from Mt. Sneffels in Iceland to Mt. Stromboli in Italy through the center of the earth!
But who ever will believe it?

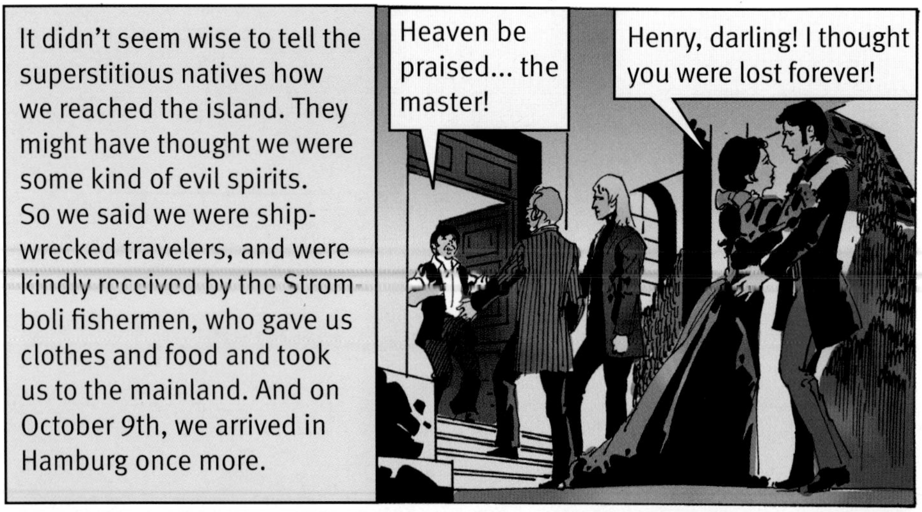
It didn't seem wise to tell the superstitious natives how we reached the island. They might have thought we were some kind of evil spirits. So we said we were ship-wrecked travelers, and were kindly received by the Strom-boli fishermen, who gave us clothes and food and took us to the mainland. And on October 9th, we arrived in Hamburg once more.
Heaven be praised... the master!
Henry, darling! I thought you were lost forever!

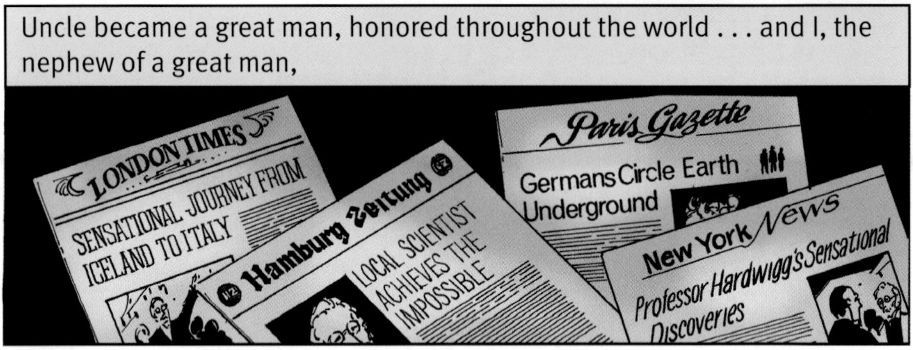
Uncle became a great man, honored throughout the world . . . and I, the nephew of a great man,
LONDON TIMES
SENSATIONAL JOURNEY FROM ICELAND TO ITALY
Hamburg Zeitung
LOCAL SCIENTIST ACHIEVES THE IMPOSSIBLE
Paris Gazette
Germans Circle Earth Underground
New York News
Professor Hardwigg's Sensational Discoveries

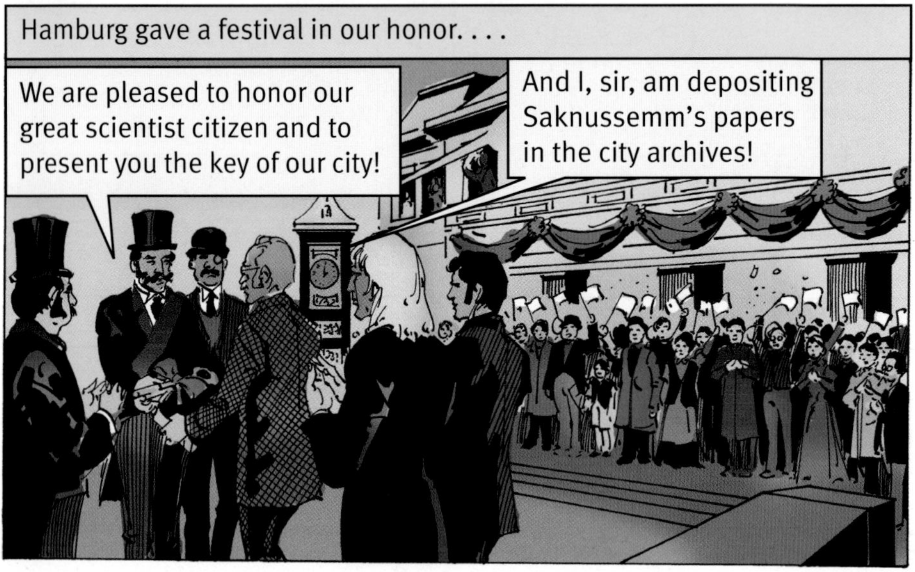
Hamburg gave a festival in our honor. . . .
We are pleased to honor our great scientist citizen and to present you the key of our city!
And I, sir, am depositing Saknussemm's papers in the city archives!

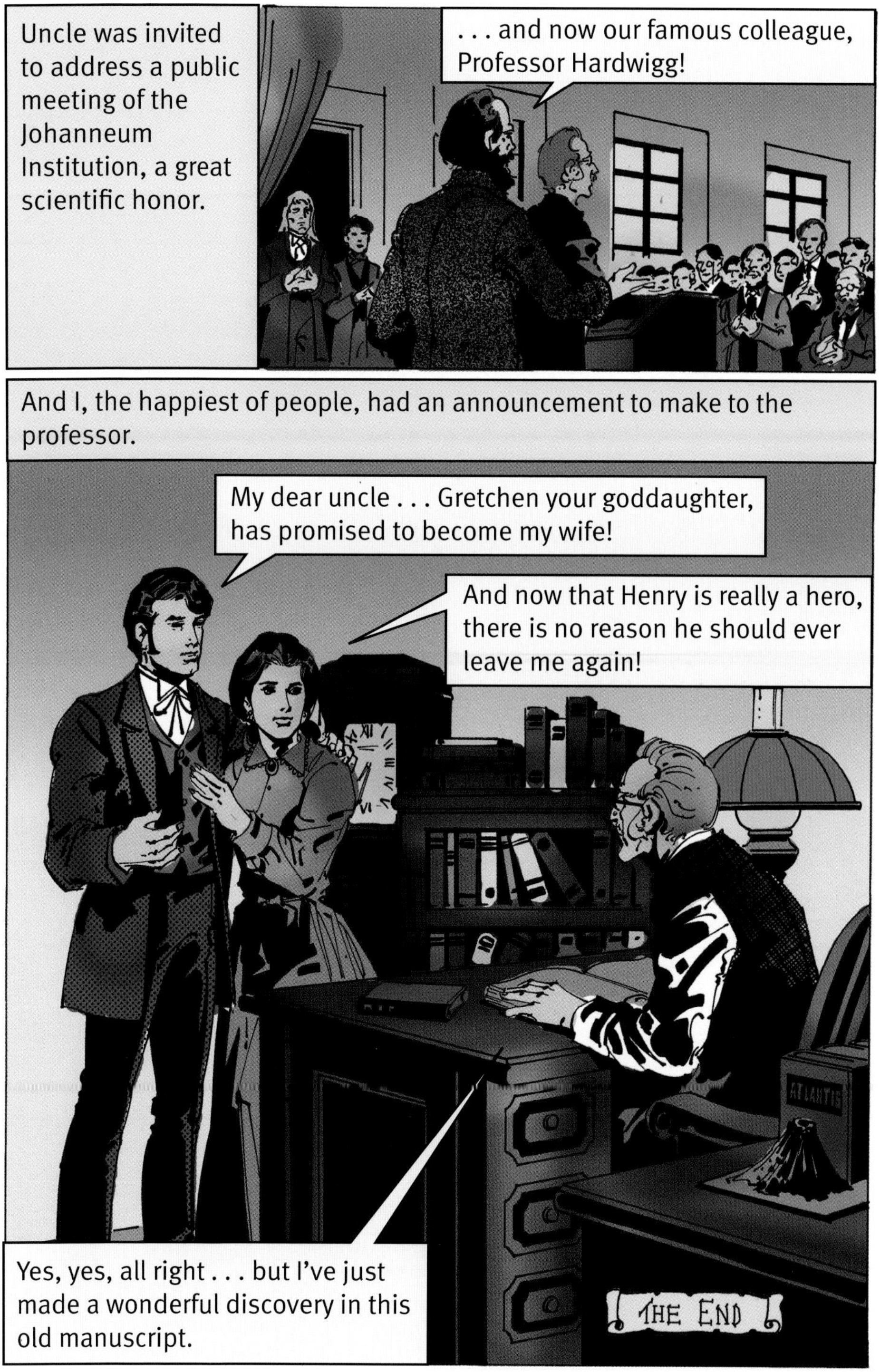
Uncle was invited to address a public meeting of the Johanneum Institution, a great scientific honor.
. . . and now our famous colleague, Professor Hardwigg!
And I, the happiest of people, had an announcement to make to the professor.
My dear uncle . . . Gretchen your goddaughter, has promised to become my wife!
And now that Henry is really a hero, there is no reason he should ever leave me again!
Yes, yes, all right . . . but I've just made a wonderful discovery in this old manuscript.
THE END